CW00515626

HEARTS ON MICHAELA

Dixie Lynn Dwyer

MENAGE EVERLASTING

Siren Publishing, Inc.
www.SirenPublishing.com

A SIREN PUBLISHING BOOK
IMPRINT: Ménage Everlasting

HEARTS ON FIRE 2: MICHAELA
Copyright © 2014 by Dixie Lynn Dwyer

ISBN: 978-1-62741-870-6

First Printing: September 2014

Cover design by Les Byerley
All art and logo copyright © 2014 by Siren Publishing, Inc.

ALL RIGHTS RESERVED: This literary work may not be reproduced or transmitted in any form or by any means, including electronic or photographic reproduction, in whole or in part, without express written permission.

All characters and events in this book are fictitious. Any resemblance to actual persons living or dead is strictly coincidental.

Printed in the U.S.A.

PUBLISHER
Siren Publishing, Inc.
www.SirenPublishing.com

DEDICATION

Dear Readers,

Thank you for legally purchasing this copy of *Hearts on Fire*. As Treasure Town continues to grow, so do the stories of the community and the people who live there. Once a hidden location, a secret amongst the locals, Treasure Town and all its people are like no others. When someone is in need, or just needs a friend, there's always someone there to offer. Michaela comes to this town with a heavy heart, a distrust of everyone, and a desire to survive, remain hidden, and avoid human contact. Her past hardens her heart and makes her question even good intentions. It takes the residents of Treasure Town and three very sexy, special men, who themselves have experienced betrayal and loss, to help her to trust again. May you enjoy her journey as a survivor, a self-empowered woman capable of loving and learning that no matter what life throws at you, each of us has the power, the inner strength, and determination to trudge on.

Happy reading,

Hugs!

~Dixie~

HEARTS ON FIRE 2: MICHAELA

DIXIE LYNN DWYER
Copyright © 2014

Prologue

"You think I won't kill her? You think I can't? I'll fucking do it!" the guy who'd just grabbed Michaela yelled toward the deputies. His grip was tight around her midsection.

She cried out as he grabbed her and not one of the other women nearby. Like maybe the snappy secretary who kept batting her eyes at the officers walking in and out of the main area.

No, instead he chose Michaela. This was a damn police department. How the hell could something like this be happening here?

Michaela Smitt was amongst the civilians, not a cop, not working undercover. She was just trying to get the legal documentation to have an abandoned vehicle removed from the small house she'd just brought. There was no title, the owner was deceased and didn't leave the car to anyone, but the tow truck company wouldn't take the vehicle without clearance from the owner, or a title. She was told that the police could help, and she showed up by their request to sign some papers.

She'd only moved here a week ago. New Jersey by the shore was supposed to be peaceful. She was also trying to stay under the radar, which right now, Alonso, her good friend and detective working her case back in New York, would not be too happy with the situation.

Well shit, neither am I.

At least one good thing happened so far today. She interviewed for a job as a bartender for a local place in town that did a lot of business called The Station. The owner, Burt McCurran, hired her on the spot. He was a burly older man with an Irish brogue and a great sense of humor. He took a liking to her immediately. She should have stayed there and enjoyed an 11:00 a.m. drink with some of the patrons.

She didn't need the job, but she needed to work to keep her mind off of New York, and the fact that she nearly died. Now here she was being held by gunpoint as she waited for the damn sheriff to arrive because the snotty secretary said he had updated information on the owner of the vehicle. It was another problem that would hold her up from getting the hunk of junk out of her driveway.

With the barrel of a gun pointed at her, for the second time in six months, Michaela was feeling like surviving was just temporary, and now she would meet her maker.

"You don't want to do that, Leonard," someone stated, and when Leonard turned her to the right, she locked gazes with a drop-dead, halt-in-your-tracks gorgeous man in uniform. He was tall, over six feet that would put her five feet five inches to shame. He had brown hair, some blonde streaks and a wide chest and shoulders that had him stepping through the doorway sideways. He even had to duck a little and perhaps her initial estimate of his height was short a few inches. He looked pissed off, and he was the only one not holding a gun. But his uniform was different than the other officers'. She stared at his gun, and it remained in the holster on his hip where his hands sat as if he casually planned on negotiating with the jerk holding her.

"I'm not going to jail, Sheriff," the man said, and she could smell the alcohol on his breath. She cringed from the smell. He didn't look like he was fully with it. She had noticed him standing next to a deputy the moment she was asked to sit and wait for the sheriff. The deputy had just uncuffed him as the man spoke with someone by another desk who was smiling and laughing. He obviously was pretending to cooperate.

"Let her go, Leonard, and we can go into my office and talk this through. There's no reason to hurt anyone. You'll regret it," the sheriff said.

"They lie. They all lie. I didn't do a thing wrong. I don't belong here. I wasn't bothering anyone." Leonard had become agitated quickly. His grip on Michaela tightened, his hand moved higher and an inch more and he would be cupping her breast. As it was now, he was awfully close.

The sheriff must have read her thoughts as he squinted his eyes and appeared as if he were losing patience. "Release the woman and we'll talk."

"Fuck you!" Leonard yelled, pulling her backward and toward another room. Her low-heeled sandals scraped across the flooring as she gripped his forearm to stop from falling. She damned the stupid blouse and camisole she wore as it spread wider, by the man's hold, giving a good view to all officers watching. She was not small up top by far, and could practically feel the cool air from the air-conditioned room hit the cleavage of her breasts. The skirt she wore fell just above her knees, but by the way he held her, she had to be showing off more thigh than she was comfortable with.

She swallowed hard as he hit the wall behind him and she nearly lost her footing. The sheriff and the deputies inched their way closer, but still kept a distance.

"Where are you gonna go, Leonard? There's nowhere to go. Let's talk about this."

"No. There's nothing to talk about. If you come closer, I'll shoot her. I don't care anymore." But now his voice sounded shaky. It seemed to her that the man was out of his mind or even high on something besides alcohol. Not that she was an expert, but she had been shot before, trying to keep a relationship with her estranged sister.

Annette was dead because of some asshole who knew Annette's boyfriend, Solomon. Solomon owed the asshole money. A lot of money. But she couldn't think about that now. Instead she thought about the training she took after recovering from the bullet wound to her chest that nearly killed her.

Alonso was a self-defense trainer. He had helped her to try and get over her anxiety and fear of being assaulted again so she could return to her real home in Chicago. But nearly dying changed a person. So she cashed in on her investments, quit her job, sold her apartment and moved out here to New Jersey. It was a place that was supposed to be quiet, peaceful, and relaxing, with the benefits of ocean and beaches. That was when she started to feel angry. She promised herself that she would never be a victim again, and now if she had the opportunity, she would use one of those moves Alonso taught her to save herself. After all, she couldn't trust anyone, not even this room filled with cops whose job was to protect and serve the public.

His hold suddenly got tighter, and now he was leaning his forehead against the back of her head, and inhaling deeply.

"What are you doing?" she asked in a rather calm tone, considering the intensity of the situation. Leonard, as the sheriff called him, seemed to be losing his composure.

He growled. "I fucking hate cops. I was having fun. I wasn't bothering anyone. I like to party, do you?" he asked and then began to slowly rotate his hips against her ass. She tried pulling away and he raised the gun as the cops and sheriff yelled for her not to move.

"Don't. Just remain still, miss. Leonard, you need to put down the gun and stop this. We don't want anyone to get hurt, and I know you don't want that either," the sheriff said. He was a little closer now, and she could see how big and tall he really was. Plus, he had amazing blue eyes. He really was a very attractive man.

"Maybe I do want to make things worse. Maybe I'm pissed off and I want to blow off some steam." Leonard antagonized the sheriff's efforts to talk him into giving up the gun.

"I want you to drop the gun, Leonard. You were brought in on drunk driving and disorderly conduct. Now, don't go turning this into a worse situation for yourself."

He adjusted his hold on her, pressing his palm over her hip bone. She gasped as a small high pitch sound got caught in her throat. She was trying so hard to not have flashbacks. She even tried remembering Alonso's instruction during training about keeping calm, and not making a move unless it was completely necessary. How would she know when making a move to get free was necessary? Right now, with him practically massaging her hip bone and pressing his privates against her ass, she felt it was necessary to get the hell away from Leonard.

"What do you think, darling? Do you think I should let you go and listen to the sheriff?" he whispered against her ear. His voice, his stench bothered her, made her think of New York, and of the thug who killed her sister. She could feel his body shaking. He was definitely on something and it seemed to be kicking in full force. He wasn't thinking clearly, and she feared for her life as the gun he held near her neck shook as hard as his hand was shaking.

He pressed his palm down her thigh making her skirt lift. "Hey!" she yelled out.

He pressed the gun harder against her neck. She tilted her head back against his shoulder, and he maneuvered his hand down the side of her thigh and up the skirt.

"Stop touching her," the sheriff yelled, and even she sensed his anger, his patience diminishing.

She took a deep breath as he showed off her bare thigh for all to see. Her breasts were definitely showing through the open blouse, and she panicked, afraid of what would happen next.

"I think you should let me go and give yourself up before you get hurt," she told him.

He lowered the gun slightly so he could use that hand with the gun to push her blouse further open. He was staring at her breasts, licking his lips.

He chuckled. "Get hurt? By whom?" he asked as he slowly moved his other hand up her waist and cupped her breast. The man lost focus and she would use the opportunity.

The sheriff yelled out, the deputies were pointing their guns at him.

"By me." She made her move.

Michaela maneuvered out of his hold, twisted his wrist around with one hand using a wrist control move Alonso taught her. She kneed him in the spine sending him down to his knees before taking his legs out from underneath him. She had the gun to the back of his head and him pinned to the ground with her straddling his legs, her skirt nearly up to her waist.

"Don't move, Leonard, or we'll see if this gun is loaded."

The sheriff and the deputies were there in a flash, taking Leonard into custody as the sheriff helped her up.

She handed him the gun.

"What the hell did you think you were doing? You could have been killed," he questioned as he held her upper arm and stared down at her chest and then her eyes.

This close, the sheriff was huge. She actually felt intimidated and tried taking a step back.

She pulled her arm free and then adjusted her blouse to cover her exposed flesh.

"I saw an opportunity and I took it before he could continue to molest me in front of an audience. Oh, and you're welcome, Sheriff."

She started walking away and noticed the other deputies looking her over and smiling. Some were shaking their heads as if they couldn't believe what she just did. Then she heard his stern voice.

"Not so fast, miss. You were just involved in a hostage situation and I need some information from you."

She turned to look at him.

"I was sitting here for over an hour waiting to be assisted. You can wait while I use a restroom and try to recover from what just went down. Then I'll talk." She stormed out of there hearing whistles at her temper, but she didn't care. That damn sheriff was a jerk.

As she spotted the sign that indicated the right door, she pushed it open and headed inside.

She looked in the mirror and saw how red her cheeks were, and felt how fast her heart was racing. Now that it was over, she was coming down off the adrenaline rush and she began to physically shake.

She had let her anger, her frustration, and mostly her fear from the past make her decisions for her. She could have been killed if she hadn't made that wrist control move so quickly. Michaela covered her mouth as she swallowed the cry that wanted to escape.

She wasn't weak. She refused to have fear. She was alone in this world with no one but herself to count on, and that was the way it had to be.

* * * *

Sheriff Jake McCurran stood with his arms crossed, waiting outside of the ladies' room. He was beside himself with shock at what just took place in his damn department. The deputy, a rookie, was being reprimanded by the sergeant while Jake waited to speak with the hostage. A woman he had surely never seen before and who also made quite the first impression.

The woman was new in town from what his secretary, Joyce, had told him. She had purchased the old Fenniger home at the end of Burgon Point. That place needed a shitload of work done to it. He wondered whom she was and all he could find out was that she came from Chicago. She was definitely capable of handling herself, but she should have let him resolve that situation. He could understand her need to defend herself as Leonard took advantage and began to fondle her. It pissed him off, immediately made him see red, as Leonard touched her.

She was a good-looking woman. Young, maybe in her twenties, and she was built well. The guys were all standing around waiting to find out who she was and whether or not she was single. Jackasses. She was just a victim and now they wanted to hit on her.

Just then the door to the restroom opened and the woman came out. Her blouse was buttoned further up than before and he felt the bit of disappointment. He cleared his head, the one on his shoulders, and reminded himself that he'd just made fun of his staff for wanting to hit on the woman.

"Miss?"

She locked gazes with him, looking straight up into his eyes. She was a petite thing compared to him. She had long brown hair and deep blue eyes, and the prettiest face he had ever seen.

"Your name?"

"Michaela."

He reached out his hand.

"Sheriff McCurran. Would you please follow me into my office?"

"Is it safe?" she asked. At first he thought she needed reassurance, but as she started walking ahead of him, he realized it was a wiseass comment. The woman had spunk, add that to the list.

"So you came here to get the documents you needed to remove the car from your new property. Sorry I wasn't here to meet you right away. I had a situation downstairs."

"I assume it wasn't as intense as the 'situation' upstairs with Leonard."

He eyed her over as she sat in a chair in front of his desk, legs crossed, eyes filled with attitude and fire. And he noticed she was shaking and hadn't accepted his offer of something to drink. She clasped her hands and started moving her foot. She was nervous, perhaps still recovering from the incident.

"Listen, if you can just give me the paperwork so that the tow truck can remove the vehicle that would be great. I can get the hell out of here and head home to all the work the place needs."

"I can't do that. When we processed the request, it came up as still being owned by Mr. Fenniger."

She sat forward. "What? How can that be when Mr. Fenniger is dead?" she asked.

"Something to do with his estate and lawyers, I guess."

"I swear if that damn thing ran, I would drop it somewhere a few towns over." She shook her head and then lowered her eyes.

"Now that would be illegal." He winked after she looked at him incredulously and chuckled.

She shook her head. "Okay, I really need to get going. I was hoping to start working on the house on Monday. The car is in the way of the Dumpster I ordered. What can I do to get this moving?"

"A Dumpster? You gutting the place?"

"Sort of."

"Who's doing the work?" he asked.

"Someone from the area. Listen, I really need to go. I have to get ready for work and still need to get back to the house. What is the next step?" she asked.

He stared at her, and he couldn't deny the attraction he felt. He wondered if she felt it, too. If she did, she wasn't giving any indication of it at all. Usually women saw the uniform and went all flirty on him. This woman seemed as if she could care less or perhaps was even turned off by his profession. Could she have some sort of past run-in with the law? When she first entered his office, she was pissed off and snappy. But she was also ready to bolt. Maybe she was just shy. She was new to town.

"Let me see what I can do. If there is a way to get it taken care of, I'll do it. Being the sheriff and growing up around here, I pretty much know everyone. I'll be in touch. Is this all your contact information?" he asked, looking over the documents she'd filled out. It would have to be filed with the charges against Leonard.

"Yes. My cell phone is best to reach me at. Thank you." She stood up and reached out her hand for him to shake. Of course he did, and as their hands touched, he was shocked by the attraction as well as the size of her small hand in his much larger one.

"See you soon."

She gave a small smile, pulling her hand from his, and then exited the room.

He glanced out between the blinds and saw the deputies saying good-bye and trying to stop her so she would talk to them, but she just smiled and waved, practically running for the exit.

He hoped to see her again, and even though he could take care of the problem with the car with one phone call, he planned on taking care of it personally and making a trip out to her new home. He wanted to see her again. She was that beautiful. He felt the slight ache in his chest and he shouldn't.

Their relationship with Lisa was over for three years now. It was time for him and his brothers, Billy and Hal, to move on.

Chapter 1

It had been a stressful few days. She had spoken to Alonso after the incident at the sheriff's department on Thursday. He wanted to call the sheriff and give him the heads-up on her case, and of course, Michaela begged him not to.

They talked about the job she took as a bartender for Thursday and Friday nights just for fun and to take her mind off of the case. He assured her that she was safe where she was and that there hadn't been any sign of Carlucci, who they believed hired the hit man who shot her. Solomon, Annette's boyfriend, who'd disappeared following the shooting, was still missing. They didn't know if Solomon was dead or alive. Nor was there any indication that either man would come looking for her. She had been a victim caught in the middle of a violent crime.

Why she even left Chicago to try to help her sister, she'll never know. It was her last try at saving Annette from the addiction. She thought about where both of them had wound up, Annette six feet under, and Michaela starting a new life in New Jersey but still unable to trust a soul except for Alonso.

Deep down, she hoped that both men did show up. Dead.

She couldn't understand why Carlucci or Solomon would want to contact her. Carlucci wasn't even officially being investigated. The detectives working the case believed that Carlucci, or a close affiliate, hired the man to kill Annette. That person, if identified and caught, would be charged in connection to the murder of her sister, and for the attempted murder of Michaela. The detectives were also searching for Solomon, the piece of shit weasel, as an accessory to murder or at minimum a witness to the crime. The jerk left his own girlfriend there to die. Michaela, too. She knew she didn't like the guy the moment her sister introduced them to one another.

But weeks after she was shot, her apartment was ransacked, and it looked as if someone was searching for something. Then five weeks later when she was past recovery and trying to get her life back on track, someone ransacked her apartment again and this time left a message saying that they would be back.

As Alonso investigated the case, they became friends, and he started helping her get over her fears and to physically as well as mentally train her. He was a wonderful man and a great person. She smiled just thinking about him and then laughed. They had thought about dating, but it didn't work out. They realized after one kiss that they were better off as friends.

Her first weekend working at The Station had been a lot of fun. Surrounded by first responders, mostly firefighters and EMS workers, she laughed a lot and found their professions admirable. So many men had also never hit on her in one night. She was a bit surprised to find out that the sheriff's father owned the place along with his longtime partner, Jerome.

Burt McCurran found out about the incident at the sheriff's department and had a chuckle over what she had done. She, however, was hoping to avoid being noticed, and her plan to stay under the radar blew up in her face. Now here she was trying to make the small, near-condemnable house into a home. But she was good at handiwork like this. She had learned a lot from her father years ago and his construction business, long before his alcoholism and disability took his life.

Sighing, she pulled back the last layer of crappy Sheetrock and stared around at the mess. She wished that damn Dumpster was closer to the house, but since the abandoned car still remained in the driveway and she hadn't heard from the sheriff with a resolution, she had to haul all the scrap to the road. Just her luck.

At this rate she wouldn't need to find a gym to join.

Michaela pulled the wiring from between the beams and gathered it along the way to the outlet. The wires were crap, the outlet needed to be replaced, and electrical work was not something to take lightly. She knew basics, but as she pulled the wires from the connection, knowing she had shut off the power box downstairs that supplied power to this area, she was shocked when it sparked.

It sounded like little firecrackers going off, and soon the damn thing was on fire, spreading a thin line up the wall the rest of the length of the wire she just pulled.

"Fuck!" she yelled out as she slammed the hammer against the wire, trying to stop it from igniting. That wouldn't work, so she reached back and pulled the small fire extinguisher from the bag of supplies she'd just bought at the local Home Depot. She peeled off the plastic covering, cursing a mile a minute as it wouldn't budge so she bit into the plastic, spit out pieces, and bit into it again as the flames increased.

"I don't need this shit." She just got the plastic off and aimed the fire extinguisher at the small fire when she heard the voice.

"Oh shit."

She had been spraying the flames, putting them out, but as she heard the voice, she turned, her hand still squeezing the device and shot the sheriff with the chemical.

"What the hell!" he yelled out, covering his head and ducking around the corner.

She had stopped pretty quickly but not quickly enough to avoid getting the stuff on his shirt and his pants.

"I'm so sorry," she exclaimed, half looking over her shoulder, making sure the fire was extinguished and half cringing from shooting the sheriff with the stuff.

"Are you okay?" he asked her, walking closer to her. She was still holding the fire extinguisher, and the sheriff was wearing regular clothing, not his uniform. He looked incredible. She pressed her hand down her dusty shorts, self-conscious about her outfit. Standing up, she realized how much taller the man was in comparison to her.

His arm muscles were huge, his chest wide and intimidating, and his hands extra large as they slowly took the canister from her hands.

"I'll take that. What the heck happened?" he asked, looking at the damage as he set the extinguisher down near the doorway and brushed off his black camo pants. Her eyes had a mind of their own as they trailed over his ass, snug and sexy in the military pants. Was he in the military at some point? Or was he a wannabe? She wondered.

"The freaking place is wired all shitty. I disconnected the power from the circuit box downstairs, but I guess it is labeled wrong or just all messed up."

"You need some help figuring that out?"

She stared at him with her hands on her hips as he looked her over. She was glad that the tank top covered her scar along her chest. She didn't want to get asked all the questions, and she wasn't going to tell anyone what had happened.

"What are you doing here?" she asked with a bit more attitude than she intended.

"I came by to let you know that I took care of the car situation. Got the title right here, and you can get it towed out first thing Monday morning. I wrote down a name of a friend of mine in town who has a tow truck service." He handed her the paper. When she took it from his hand, he held hers firmly a second longer.

He glanced around the place as she looked over the letter.

"This is great. I wish it came earlier though. I had to have the Dumpster parked in the road."

"No one complained, did they?" he asked.

"The neighbors? No way, they seem thrilled that I'm going to clean up the place. It is an eyesore with no curb appeal."

"Why did you buy this place?" he asked, looking around the room. He trailed his hand along the wood railing that separated the entryway from the living room.

"I think it has charm, or at least will have it when I'm finished."

"I thought you said you hired someone to do the renovations."

"I said the person was local. It's me." She took the letter and placed it in a drawer by a desk that was neatly set up by the front hallway. She had done that area first, wanted to do the living room and then the kitchen. Hopefully the bedrooms after that.

"You're doing the construction yourself?"

She crossed her arms in front of her chest, not even realizing she made her boobs stand out more until the sheriff's eyes grazed her cleavage and then looked up toward her face.

"I know what I'm doing."

"Didn't seem that way when I got here," he teased and winked.

She shook her head. "Totally not my fault, but it's to be expected in a dump this old."

"How about the circuit box? You need help labeling it so something like this doesn't happen again?"

"I can handle it. Thanks."

"How can you check and label if the circuit breaker box is in the basement and all the rooms and lights are upstairs?"

Duh, he was right. She couldn't. "You don't need to be anywhere else right now?"

"Nope. I'm off today, but I know how desperate you were to get rid of the car."

"I appreciate that. Let me just grab something to label the switches with. You can turn the stuff on and yell down to me."

"I think I'll bring along this fire extinguisher," he said and winked.

* * * *

It had taken them a good thirty minutes to label all the circuits and secure them. It had given Jake an opportunity to try and see who Michaela was. She didn't have a lot of belongings, but she did have books out on renovating old homes and other things like that, and her bedroom was meticulous. He could smell the fresh paint on the walls, and what looked like a work in progress of a mosaic on one wall of the room. Whatever it was going to be, it was already impressive.

"Hey, who did this painting?" he called down to her again, as she said they had gotten the last switch identified.

He heard her footsteps as she climbed the old staircase. He noticed she had a book on restoring that as well.

"What did you ask?" She stood in the doorway but didn't enter. He motioned with his hand.

"This, whose painting is this?" he asked.

She walked in, but she appeared guarded, as she uncrossed her arms.

"Oh, it's nothing, just something I've been working on."

"You painted this?" he asked and then squatted down to view the bottom half of the scene. "It looks like something from Italy."

He glanced up at her and she squinted her eyes and looked unimpressed. She obviously was a hard critic of her own work. Her talent, and also her ability to take on the house in its condition, impressed him.

"What, you don't think so?" he asked, standing back up.

"It's nowhere near completion. It was just an idea I had in my head. I might paint over it anyway." She headed out of the room.

"Don't even think of doing that. It's really good, Michaela. How long have you been painting for?"

She rubbed her left arm, something she seemed to do whenever he asked her something personal. It seemed to be a nervous twitch. But what would a young, beautiful woman like Michaela need to be worried about?

"It doesn't matter. I have so much to do with this house. And now it seems like I might need an electrician." He followed her out of the bedroom and down the narrow hallway. Up here, she looked really petite in comparison to him. And young. Too damn young if he could resist her beauty and interest.

Her long brown hair was pulled into two braided pigtails, making her seem even more youthful, but a gaze over her round, full ass, slender hips, and of course her large breasts, and he knew damn well she wasn't too young. Her personality, physical appearance, and more natural beauty, were the complete opposite of Lisa.

He felt only a slight tinge of guilt and sadness thinking of her at the moment and comparing her to Michaela. They were so different and he couldn't think of one thing so far that the two women had in common.

Lisa was high maintenance, high class, with money and a need for the best. He and his brothers fell for her acting job about them being meant for one another. It hadn't been until they were in bed with her and her insistence that they do things with other people that it hit home. She wanted an orgy, not a committed ménage relationship. She thought it was sexy and fun, and it took catching her in bed with two other men for them to realize she'd scammed them. But they cared about her. They had trusted her and gave her their hearts and she stomped on them and destroyed the whole meaning behind a ménage relationship.

Then they tried working things out and they got back together.

Then she hit them with the best and worst news ever as they battled in yet another argument over her wants and desires. He cringed from the memory of her words as they struck through his heart and his brothers'.

"Would you like some ice tea?" Michaela interrupted his thoughts.

He shook the bad memories from his head as he followed her into the kitchen.

"Sure. Thank you."

He looked around the kitchen and saw the same thing as the other rooms. It needed work but had actually been in better shape than he thought it would be.

"What're your plans for in here?" he asked as she poured them each a glass of ice tea and then joined him by the kitchen table.

She looked around the room. "Well, I really haven't decided yet. I was thinking of taking that wall behind you down, opening up the kitchen and living room, figuring that would be good for entertaining."

"You have a large family?" he asked, and saw the color drain from her face. It was obvious his question shocked her.

"No. I think it would be great for resale value."

"Resale value? You're not sticking around here?" he asked, feeling disappointed, and he made that pretty obvious as he nearly choked on the sip of tea. No woman ever made him react like this. It was unnerving.

"Eventually, maybe. I don't know. I think it's a nice town, Sheriff. The people seem friendly and your father's bar, The Station, is pretty cool."

"Jake, please call me Jake."

"Jake." She eyed him over the glass before she turned away.

"I heard that you were working at The Station. How do you like it so far?"

"I like it. It's busy and the tips are great. Firefighters can get pretty rowdy."

"Can't we all."

She chuckled. "Well, again, I appreciate you helping me out." She stood up and he knew she wanted him to leave, but why? They were getting along fine.

"Kicking me out?" he asked as he stared at her while running his fingertip around the rim of the ice tea glass.

"It's your day off, I'm sure you have much better things to do than hang out here with me where you could get electrocuted, sprayed with chemicals, or put to work."

"I don't mind at all. I have actually enjoyed our time together. It's the best way to get to know someone."

She placed her glass into the sink, and turned to stare at him.

The sunlight cast a nice gentle glow over her body, and especially her hair that sparkled with red and golden highlights.

"Listen, Sheriff, Jake, I appreciate the gesture. You handling my car situation, and you coming over here helping me, but I'm kind of used to being alone. In fact I prefer to be alone."

He stared at her as he stood up. He walked his glass to the sink and now she stood right by him. Her lower back was leaning against the counter.

He stood in front of her, looking down into her big blue eyes, and he reached up to move a strand of hair from her cheek.

"Being alone can be peaceful, but it's also lonely. You're new in town, could use a friend, if something comes up that you need. I'd like to be there for you."

She squinted her eyes at him. "I'm not interested in making any friends, Jake. I appreciate you coming by and dropping off the paperwork. I'll be sure to call the tow service you recommended on Monday." She stepped away and he had no choice but to follow her from the kitchen. He sensed her anxiety as he invaded her space. She didn't move right away, but she felt the attraction as he had. Why was she so resistant, and what was with the "I don't need to make friends" remark?

She opened her front door and held it open for him.

"Well, good luck with the house. I can give you the names of a few trustworthy electricians if you need help?"

"I'm good."

He looked her over and she cleared her throat as she stepped back across the threshold and into the safety of her home.

He winked before he headed down the walkway and to his truck. He wondered if she were still watching him. If she was, then maybe she was just shy and he had come off too aggressive. He glanced over his shoulder and waved as she pretended to look inside of her mailbox attached to the house.

Yeah, she was interested, but for some reason she was resistant. He wondered why as he got into his truck and headed home.

Chapter 2

"Well, where the hell could she have gone, Clyde?" Solomon asked. "It's not like she has any family left. Annette told me their parents were dead." He spoke into the phone, listening to Clyde Duvall. The man was supposed to be a great tracker. Solomon was paying him well to find Michaela and locate the key to the safety deposit box.

"I don't know. I need more time. It's like she disappeared after she recovered from the hospital in New York. I had my people look into her residence in Chicago, and one day it was vacated, items were sold off or donated. The landlord didn't have any information."

Solomon was shacked up in a shit apartment downtown, and he could just imagine Clyde, standing in his executive office uptown.

Solomon was impressed with Clyde's office. It overlooked the city of Manhattan. Solomon was hoping for a position in a firm that Clyde chaired and owned the majority of stocks in, but after the incident with Carlucci, and the fact that Solomon knew Carlucci hired the hit man who killed Annette, his hopes of staying alive in America were slim to none.

He needed the key that Annette had hidden for him. There were fake passports so he could get out of the country, a shitload of money so he could survive on his own, and the thumb drive that Carlucci wanted so badly. There was enough evidence on that thumb drive to put Carlucci and his organization away for life, and prove that he hired the hit man to kill Solomon but instead wound up killing Annette and nearly killing her sister, Michaela. Plus, certain political opponents would pay for that information so Carlucci wouldn't have a chance of winning his reelection. That was what the other thumb drives were for. A reserve to ensure he remained alive. People would kill for the information on those thumb drives.

He kind of felt bad for Michaela. She survived, but had no idea what she had gotten caught up in. Carlucci could be looking for her right now to finish the job, or at minimum, track down Solomon.

"If I find her, what do you want me to do?"

"Call me first. If I can get to you easy, then I'll take care of the rest. If I can't, then you may have to hold her up somewhere until I retrieve what I need."

"What does she have that you need so badly? You're taking a chance sticking around here when the cops are looking for you and the guy who killed your girlfriend."

"I just need something she has before I ditch this place. Plus, I'd like nothing more than to see Carlucci dead."

"Which is why I'm helping you out. I'm not going to lie to you, Solomon. It would serve some of my own interests to get rid of that slimy bastard."

Solomon smiled to himself. This was what he had hoped for. If he needed to get out of the country, then he could give Clyde a copy of the thumb drive and let him deliver the dirty work.

"I understand. The man has rubbed a lot of people the wrong way. I don't know why the majority of people can't see through his bullshit. If they only knew what he was into."

"Sounds like you have some shit on him. If you need a partner in this, I'm in. What do you have? Photographs, confiscated files from his personal computer? What?" Clyde asked.

"No specifics, Clyde. But I have a bunch of shit on thumb drives hidden in a safe location."

"So this chick I'm tracking knows where these thumb drives are? No wonder you're worried that Carlucci's man might find her first. Is it in a security box somewhere? I sure hope so for your sake. Carlucci has a lot of pull and connections everywhere."

"Money and power can bring a person a long way. Listen, call me next week or I'll find a way to contact you if I get any updates on the woman. Be safe."

Clyde disconnected the call and Solomon turned off the disposable phone so it couldn't be tracked. He knew that Clyde had his own interests in helping him. It paid to have friends in some shitty positions, and Solomon knew that Clyde wanted Carlucci out of the race.

It was why he called him for help with tracking down Michaela. In fact, his only other problem would be Michaela and what to do with her after he got what he wanted from her.

Well, he had time to make that plan, but for both their sakes, he hoped he was the one to find her and not Carlucci's hit man.

* * * *

Hal was getting ready for work at the firehouse when his brother Jake walked into their home.

"Where have you been?" Hal asked, and Jake raised his eyebrow at him.

Jake placed a bag onto the counter with a sandwich he brought at the deli after leaving Michaela's house. He was tempted to pick her up something, too, and go back as a peace offering. But then thought better of it. She might think he was stalking her. Truth was he couldn't stop thinking about her. She wasn't just another good-looking woman. She seemed tough, authentic, and also resistant. Her words about not needing to make friends sat heavy on his heart. He couldn't help but to wonder if someone hurt her.

"I was out, had to run a few errands, and then grabbed lunch."

"Are you sure you're feeling okay? You're not still upset about the situation at the police station and how that woman took action?"

Jake placed his hands on the counter, palms down, and stared at his brother. Hal was just as tall as him but not as bulky. He was trim, all muscle, and had blonder hair. Where Jake's was light brown with blond highlights.

"No, I'm not still upset about that."

"Okay. Just making sure. Because I did notice you bench pressing a little lighter yesterday and maybe thought that you were losing your confidence."

Jake grabbed the dishtowel and threw it at Hal's head as Hal laughed.

"Where's Billy? He's on today, too, right?"

"Yeah, he's getting ready. He was out with Lance and Tyler last night. They were talking to some women when one of them brought up Lisa. Apparently she knew her from a yoga class or something."

Jake squinted his eyes and felt his temper rising already. Whenever Lisa's name came up it brought trouble and anger in each of them.

Just then Billy walked in.

"It was no big deal. I told you not to even mention it to Jake," Billy stated, ducking as he entered the kitchen. He was just as tall as Jake but with dark brown hair that reached his shoulders. He was a big man with lots of muscles, and appeared sort of untamed. Some of their friends called him Tarzan, but most called him by his call sign. His size and demeanor gave him the call sign Bear at work. As opposed to Hal, who they called Hollywood because he was always wearing sunglasses and sporting the latest styles for men. He took pride in his appearance and the women loved it.

"What happened?" Jake asked, now crossing his arms in front of his chest.

Hal chuckled, knowing that Jake would get the info out of him. Jake was always a good interrogator. It had come in handy many times during their stints in the service. Jake had abilities.

"It was the same stupid shit. Lisa spreading lies about us dumping her after promising marriage and a commitment."

"That bitch should just move on. What about those two ass wipes from Jersey City? I thought after she shacked up with them and we caught her, the first freaking time, that she was committed to them?" Jake asked.

"Haven't you realized that Lisa doesn't know the first thing about commitment? She's a stuck-up, rich snob who just goes with whatever the latest craze is. Over a year ago it was a ménage with us," Hal said.

"We need to move on and just put her behind us," Jake stated and then walked near the kitchen nook that looked out toward the channel. Their boat sat there and it had been weeks since they took it out. He wondered if Michaela would want to go for a ride.

"Hey, what's with you over there daydreaming?" Hal asked, giving Jake a light nudge in his shoulder.

He took a deep breath and released it.

"I think we need to move on. I think the time for finding someone we all might like, and taking another chance is now. It's been more than a year."

"Why would you want go through that bullshit again? We thought that Lisa was into the relationship we wanted. Hell, what she did to us was just totally fucked up. I put a lot into the relationship and I just don't think I have the energy or the desire to do it again," Hal stated.

"You mean you're giving up on what we decided we wanted years ago?" Jake asked.

"I don't know. It just seems rare that these types of relationships work out. I haven't even met anyone who I think is right, or that I'm willing to give it a try with," Bear added.

"Listen, I'm not saying let's go out and start hunting down a woman. I'm saying, let's be open to the possibility of moving on now. We're older, more mature, and know what we want. We can bypass the women looking for a new experience and to have a good time, and focus on the ones who understand this type of relationship or who purely, physically feel an attraction. I'm saying it's time to move on."

"I don't know if I could trust another woman again. Not after what Lisa did behind our backs and after she cheated on us like that," Bear said as he took the truck keys from his pocket and grabbed his duffel bag.

"I'm with Billy. I don't know if I'm ready to take that chance. Hell, I haven't even met anyone I could think was a possibility for me, never mind for the two of you. I think we should just stop thinking about it," Hal said. Then he grabbed his bag and the two of them said good-bye before walking from the house and leaving Jake there to think about what they said.

But as Hal walked out with Bear and headed toward Bear's truck, he couldn't help but feel that inkling of hope that maybe one day they would meet the right woman. She would have to be a trustworthy woman who didn't lie, who didn't pretend to care, and who truly loved the three of them so they could all have a future people only dreamt about.

Chapter 3

"Hey, Smiley, you sure do know how to handle a busy bar. That must have been a hell of a joint ya worked at in Chicago," Burt stated as he stood next to her behind the bar. The new nickname he gave her had started off as a wise guy remark about her serious expression. But because of it, she was smiling constantly and actually enjoying the bar, her bosses and the new nickname. Burt had been watching her, keeping a close eye on her moves, on how much alcohol she put in the drinks. It was all typical of an owner watching over his bar.

She chuckled at him. She really did get a lot of joy out of his Irish brogue. Even his partner, her other boss Jerome, had a nice accent going on.

Both men were charming, very flirty and fun, but also tough as nails. Earlier in the evening before the Friday night crowd began to pour in, Burt showed her around the place and talked to her about the memorabilia. She had a chance to see a great picture of Burt with his three sons. Three very good-looking and extra large men.

She was surprised by her reaction to the picture. The four men appeared happy, and as if they had a great relationship. She wondered about their mother, Burt's wife, but didn't want to ask. If she asked questions, then Burt would ask questions.

But her plan backfired as he told her all about Mary and how wonderful of a mother and wife she was before she died of heart disease. It was sad, but he was definitely in love with her.

Michaela had a hard childhood. She lived in a shitty neighborhood, went to even crappier schools, and had to practically live on work sites for her father's construction company. She didn't own a toy—not a doll, a bear, or even a matchbox car. Her parents were always struggling and always fighting. Her father's relationship with her mom, an alcoholic, was crappy and rocky. They fought all the time and eventually her father turned to drinking, too.

Then came his accident and his depression. Down went the business as she took care of her father while Annette took off, unable to handle a thing. Mom died, Dad followed, and Michaela learned fast about responsibility, debt, and hardship.

It took years of working in some of the craziest but highest paying clubs in Chicago to pay her parents' debt, sell the house, and begin college. But she did it. She had a knack for numbers, finished top in her class, and landed an awesome job at a big firm in the city. She tried contacting Annette, visited her a few times, and even helped support her so she could get her life on track, but then she met Solomon.

Why did I ever go to New York to see her when she basically told me to forget about her?

"Hey, Smiley, meet my son Hal," Burt stated, giving her elbow a nudge and bringing her back to the present. The night crew was beginning to arrive. The ladies were all dolled up and ready to land a first responder, and the guys were all rowdy.

She looked up and up, until her eyes locked gazes with the stunning man with incredibly blue eyes. His hair was not quite blond, more dirty blonde and nearly reached his shoulders but curled at the ends. It looked so smooth and shiny. She imagined women probably loved to run their fingers through it. He was absolutely gorgeous.

"Hal, meet my new bartender, Smiley."

"Darling, you can't be the little number that showed up my brother in his own sheriff's department. Wow, I'm impressed." He eyed her over from breasts to face. She felt a bit guilty for gaining such a reputation, but it seemed the incident at the sheriff's department was still fresh on people's minds and the story had been exaggerated, with the sheriff at the brunt of the jokes.

"This is her. Ain't she a gorgeous little young lassie?" Burt asked, squeezing her shoulders from behind her. She chuckled as he walked away to help another patron.

"Nice to meet you, Smiley." He reached his hand out to shake hers and she reached across the bar.

"It's Michaela. Your dad is just messing with me and the nickname thing," she said as their hands touched. She felt that instant attraction. It went straight to her gut and she pulled back, grabbing the rag and wiping down the bar.

"What are you drinking?" she asked him.

"A Bud is fine," he said, never taking is eyes off of her, and then he ran his fingers through his hair as she pulled the lever to the bar tap, filling the ice cold mug with beer.

She watched him, as she kept watch of the mug. She was right. He looked sexy running his fingers through his hair. He also looked a bit less serious than his brother, Jake.

She placed a coaster down and then the mug of beer.

"Hey, Hollywood, how's it going?" Some guy came up behind Hal and joined him by the bar. She had seen him at The Station before. She was starting to recognize the regulars.

"Hey, Tyler. What's up? How's it going?"

"Not bad. Where's Bear? I thought you two traveled by the hip," Tyler stated and then looked up at Michaela.

"Get you something?"

He eyed her over. "Sure, sweetheart. I'll take a Bud, too."

She grabbed a cold mug from the cooler and poured the beer.

"Smiley, I need three cosmos for the three young ladies at the end of the bar there, can you do that for me? They requested yours, not mine," Jerome told her. Holding his hands up in front of him as he rolled his eyes.

"I thought you liked making those girly drinks, Jerome?" Tyler teased as Michaela set down Tyler's beer and headed toward the other end of the bar. A glance over her shoulder and Hal was leaning forward as if to get a look at her backside.

She smiled to herself. Typical hotshot firefighter, out to flirt with the new girl. She was glad she knew this business well. A tight pair of jean shorts, the bar's logo tank top, just as tight and lifted slightly at the belly to reveal a hint of her tanned, toned abs along with the belly ring. She knew what got the tips, but she also knew her limitations. She could easily flaunt her size thirty-six double Ds, but that wasn't her style. Sometimes less was more.

* * * *

"So that's the new girl. Wow, she is hot," Tyler said, taking a sip from his beer, still keeping his eyes on her.

"I guess so."

Tyler gave him a shove. "Are you fucking shitting me? I saw you staring at her ass as she turned to head down the bar to make those cosmos. What does your brother Jake know about her? Any inside information?"

"Why?"

"Look at her. She's cute, has a great body, sweet smile, and doesn't flaunt her assets. Plus, everyone heard about her ability to defend herself. Your brother must have been pissed off about that, huh?" Tyler asked as he chuckled.

Hal shook his head and smirked. Jake had been steamed but not as badly as he thought his brother would be. Hal had heard about what happened at the sheriff's department. That woman was lucky she wasn't shot. But given the circumstances of the situation and the fact that some guy was groping her, he thought she reacted accordingly and had the knowledge of some self-defense to take control of the situation. He heard all about her sexy body, the skirt to her waist as she straddled the thug, pointing his gun to his head. He would have loved to see the video.

"What are you smirking about?" Tyler asked.

Hal looked back down the bar to where Smiley was talking with some other guys and the women she made the cosmos for.

"Just wishing I had the chance to see the video."

"You didn't see it? I saw it yesterday. So many people have downloaded that thing. I wouldn't be surprised if it wound up on the news or even YouTube."

"Shit, Jake is going to be pissed about that."

"Pissed about what?" Jake asked, coming up behind him. Tyler chuckled, and Hal gave him a dirty look. He could have warned him that Jake was behind him.

"Nothing."

"Bullshit, nothing. What? What would I be pissed at?" Jake asked but wasn't looking at Hal. He was looking down the bar and his eyes were locked on Smiley.

"She's one sexy little thing, isn't she, Sheriff?" Tyler teased and then walked away chuckling.

Jake gave Tyler a dirty look and then shook his head.

He took the seat next to Jake.

"What can I get you, Jake?" Jerome asked.

Jake looked down the bar to where Michaela was. She looked up and locked gazes with him. Hal watched as her face lit up and she gave a small wave. His brother nodded his head toward her, smiling.

"You'll have to wait in line for a chance with that one, Jake. There's a waiting list of men interested in Smiley," Jerome said, pulling on the lever, filling a cold mug with beer. He placed it down on the bar in front of Jake.

"A waiting list?" Hal asked Jerome. Jerome chuckled.

"Smiley? Who started that? Oh, forget I asked. My dad, right?" Jake asked.

Jerome chuckled. "Yep. He's taken a real liking to her."

"A liking to her?" Jake snapped at Jerome. Hal wondered if his brother was thinking what he was thinking. Could their dad be interested in Michaela? She was too young. Hell, she could be his damn daughter.

"You two get those damn looks off your faces. Your dad could be her damn father. Not that kind of interest. She's a sweet young woman. She keeps to herself, doesn't give much info, and your dad and I think she's hiding something. You saw the video, Jake. How many women can make moves like that without some sort of formal training?" Jerome asked as he dried a couple of beer mugs.

"What video?" Jake asked.

"He doesn't know, Jerome," Hal informed him.

"Oh shit. I'd better go down and check on Michaela, see if she needs some help." Jerome walked away and Jake looked at Hal.

"What fucking video?"

"The one from the sheriff's department. The incident was recorded and someone uploaded it to the Internet."

"Oh hell. That's not good."

"You're telling me. She snagged the attention of a few guys immediately, but now, with that video out, she'll have a lot of guys hitting on her."

"I need to talk to her. Let her know about this."

"You think Jerome is right? You think there's a waiting list?"

"She's not that kind of woman. She's sweet, quiet, doesn't want to give a lot of info on herself or any family. I spent a little time with her on Sunday. Jerome could be right. Dad's good at detecting shit like that."

"You spent time with her at her house?" Hal asked. He didn't know why but he felt both insulted and jealous, and he shouldn't be. Neither him, Bear, nor Jake had dated anyone since Lisa. It had fucked up their heads and killed their ability to trust. Especially after what they found out Lisa did. Maybe this was why his brother hinted about dating again?

"I was going to talk to you and Bear about it. It's just that the visit with her was kind of mixed. I mean, she is very attractive, and resourceful, independent, and a complete opposite of what Lisa was like."

"Don't bring up her name. I fucking hate even thinking about her."

"I know, Hal. I do, too. I was just saying that Michaela is completely different. She's tough, and she's got a shell around her. After we talked a bit and I helped her at the house, I told her I'd like to be friends and be there for her if she needs anything since she's new in town."

"And?"

"She basically shot me down, and told me she didn't need any friends. She was good on her own. Now, normally I would take that as a sign she's not interested, but I felt the attraction. I saw it in her eyes, and then they changed to an expression of fear, and it was like she threw up this wall and blew me off. I've been thinking about it all week."

He took a sip of the beer.

"All week? Why didn't you talk to Bear and I?"

"I don't know. I guess I was worried about both of your responses, maybe the possibility of being rejected by her?"

"Well you shouldn't have been. I think she's very attractive, and seems really sweet, too. Now if Bear shows up and he thinks the same, we're going to have to have a talk, and decide."

"I know. I'm just not sure I'm ready to take a chance like this again. It fucking hurt, what Lisa did to us," Jake stated with a firm expression as he glanced around the bar and looked at Michaela again. He took a sip of beer and Hal did the same. He felt the same as Jake did. Lisa fucked with their heads, and their hearts. It wasn't just the fact that she cheated on them. It was what she did prior to that without their consent and without them knowing. It wasn't something a man could forget. It left a bad taste in his mouth, and made his heart hard. Could Smiley be different? Could she possibly make them forget about Lisa even if just for a little while? Maybe she wouldn't even give them the time of day. After all, all the guys were hitting on her right now.

* * * *

Michaela was shaking her head at some flirtatious remark some guy had thrown at her. She gave a sassy reply and then continued to make the drinks until Jerome came back over. This was his side of the bar tonight, so she winked and headed back over toward the other end.

She felt that bit of butterflies in her belly at seeing Jake again. She had a hard time sleeping all week, thinking about him and his comment about being friends. She knew he liked her. Hell, she found him to be pretty damn sexy. But she was trying to keep a low profile.

When she met his brother Hal, she was surprised at how her body reacted the same way. The man was very sexy as well. Good genes must run in the family. She had seen a picture of all the McCurran men, and even the third brother, Billy, was attractive, and big, too. She had yet to meet him, but feared she would feel an attraction, too.

Something she learned quickly living around this town was that men shared their women. There were ménage relationships everywhere, and they even had families, worked regular jobs in the community, and no one seemed to care, especially not the traditional couples. That knowledge had given her some pretty interesting dreams the last few nights. But that type of life was a fantasy, a relationship she surely would fail at because of her lack of trust. There had to be some serious trust and commitment for a relationship like a ménage to work and to last.

As she cleared her head of the thoughts, she stopped to assist a few guys with their drink orders.

"So, Smiley, what do you like to do when you're not working here?" some guy Alex asked.

"Oh, I keep busy," she said, placing their beers down in front of the three men. All of them were watching her.

"Like what? What do you like to do for fun?" the other guy asked.

"Well, right now I'm working on fixing up my house. That should keep me busy day and night for quite some time. Excuse me a minute, guys." She smiled then walked a little further down the bar to see if Hal and Jake needed new beers. Theirs were getting low.

"Good evening, Sheriff. You two need two more beers?" she asked, and Hal nodded.

"Hey, I thought we discussed the whole sheriff thing the other day at your house?" he asked, saying it kind of loudly. She noticed that the guys who were flirting heard, and now they looked at Jake and Hal. Jake just gave a nod and a smile. The three men headed away from the bar. She wondered what just silently went down here as she filled the two beers and placed them next to Jake and Hal's other mugs. Both men downed the remainder in the other mugs and she removed them.

"Well, I didn't want to not show respect for your public position," she said as she stared at him. He looked good tonight. Really good, even though he was growing a little gruff along his chin and cheeks. It made him appear older, seasoned, experienced, and rather intimidating. She swallowed.

"His friends call him Jake," Hal stated. When she looked at him, he was holding the mug with his large hand as he held her gaze with his bold, blue eyes.

"I thought we discussed the whole friends thing, too." She winked.

"Sweetheart, you'll come to realize that I'm pretty damn stubborn. I want something, or I offer something, I expect the one I'm offering it to take me up on it. Now, everyone can use a friend, especially when they're new in town. So you remember that."

"Yes, Sheriff, Jake, I will."

"So, I heard you tell those guys that you're working on your house. What are you doing? Painting?"

She placed her hands on the brass bar below the shelf and started to tell Hal about dry walling, tearing down the walls, doing the electrical work, and renovating.

"Holy shit. You know how to do all that?" he asked, sounding impressed.

"Sure do, but it's a lot harder than I remember."

"Where did you learn how to do that?"

"Oh I picked it up here and there. It's not too bad, and if I get stuck, I have books I brought and collected over the years, and there's always the Internet."

"Speaking of the Internet, you and I need to talk," Jake told her.

"About what?"

"It seems that the video surveillance from my department was downloaded by a few morons, and it may or may not be running freely on the Internet."

"What?" Her heart caught in her throat, and she looked around and then tried to calm her reaction. She didn't want to let them know that this was bad. She was trying to stay low key. Shit.

"Will you excuse me, please." Before they could answer, she grabbed Jerome's arm and whispered that she needed a minute and then she hurried out the back. She was in the back room by the emergency exit door. She looked around and no one was there, so she pulled out her cell and made the call.

"Alonso, it's me. I have a potential situation."

"Again? Now what?" he teased her.

"That incident at the sheriff's department was recorded on a surveillance video and some jackass uploaded it to share with friends and it may be on the Internet."

"Oh shit. Who the hell would do that, one of the deputies?"

"I guess one of the deputies. I know the sheriff didn't do it. He just informed me now at work. What should I do? I mean, do I need to leave here? Relocate? I'm kind of worried."

"No, just calm down. The likelihood that they're still looking for you is probably slim. We haven't had any sightings at all. In fact the Feds haven't either. There is some chatter about potential political corruption that could be related to Carlucci, but considering he's dodged the whole hired hit man thing, I'd say nothing is brewing."

"What about the hit man, any word on him?"

"As far as we know, he's still out there, but his mug was sent to every police department and law enforcement agency across the United States. Maybe I should call the sheriff and give him the heads-up."

"No. The sheriff can't know. No one can. I have a bag, and things ready if I need to get out of here in a hurry. I can't believe this is happening. When is it going to be over? When am I going to get my life back and not have to live in constant fear?"

"I don't know, Michaela. I know you are scared. Listen, I need to get back to work. I'll talk to you soon."

"Take care."

"Bye."

She hung up the phone and then slammed her hand against the door.

"Michaela?"

She shot around and saw Burt standing there. He looked angry, concerned, and she realized that he had heard her phone call.

"What's going on?"

She attempted to speak and he held up his hand.

"Don't lie to me. I knew something was going on. I have an instinct for this kind of thing. You're in trouble?"

"I don't really want to talk about it, Burt. I can't tell you."

"But you're scared, and you're alone. You're hiding from someone. Was that the police?"

She looked away and started to head past him. He stopped her by gently taking her hand into his. She paused, shocked at not only how she instantly thought of Burt as a father figure, but also how quickly her heart ached for not being able to accept his help or even reassurances. She had trained herself to be resistant to everyone. But she didn't want to hurt Burt's feeling.

"I like you, Michaela. I have a natural ability to see a good person when I meet one. Whatever ya might have done won't matter to me. I can help you and all you have to do is let me. It's that simple, lassie." His brogue, his deep voice, his height and size, just like his sons seemed to have inherited from him, was enough to make her loosen her tongue.

"A detective. But please, Burt, the less you know, the better."

"You going to leave town?" he asked, releasing her arm.

She ran her hands over her face and then leaned against the wall next to the door. "I don't know. I really don't know what to do. But I can handle it. Just like I've handled everything else that's been dished out to me. I'd better get back to work or Jerome is going to give me hell," she said and smiled.

"Jerome answers to me," Burt countered as they headed out through the doorway together.

"I thought you two were partners?"

They came back to the bar and it was more crowded than before.

"We are, but I own a little more than half and that makes me the head honcho. We'll talk later." He squeezed her shoulder and gave her a wink. She smiled, thinking how nice he was, and as she turned toward the bar to take some drink orders, there were Jake, Hal, and some other big guy just staring at her and then at their father and then back at her again.

She tried to act unaffected by their stares and good looks, but it wasn't easy, the moment she heard Jake's voice.

"Michaela, come here, please." She swallowed hard and then approached where they sat.

"We thought you left," Hal stated and he seemed angry.

"No, I was just taking a call and then talking to your dad."

"It didn't look that way," the other guy stated. When she looked up toward him, standing this much closer than before, she realized who he was.

"Hey, you're the other son. Billy, right?"

"That's right, sweetheart." He reached his hand out to shake hers. As her much smaller hand was encased by his large one, she felt the tiny fluttering in her belly, and her eyes widened. She pulled away and pretended to wipe down the counter.

"Do you guys need another round?" she asked, and Hal nodded.

She walked over to pour three more beers when Jerome came by. "Are you okay? You seem a little preoccupied."

"Sure thing. I just had a call to make."

"I meant with Jake, Hal, and Billy. Those three have their eyes on you."

"Well, they can look all they want, I don't date."

"Really, because those three could use a nice girlfriend like you, instead of the snotty, two-faced—"

"What?" she found herself asking.

Jerome looked toward the guys and then back at her. "Just an old man talking stupid. I hope everything is okay. If you need a friend, I'm here for you and I know that Burt is, too."

"Thanks, Jerome." She smiled. Then she brought the three beers over toward the men. As they said thank you, another set of people ordered more drinks, and she spent the next hour catching up on drink orders and declining offers of dates and trips around town.

* * * *

Burt was getting ready to close up the place for the night. It was four o'clock in the morning, and the last few stragglers were accompanied by Jerome to their awaiting cabs home.

Jerome walked back inside and locked the door.

"Well, another Friday night gone and went. I haven't seen it this crowded in a while," Jerome stated.

"That's because of Smiley," Burt replied as Michaela turned off the lights by the bar after washing everything down and preparing the bar for tomorrow.

"That's not true. Stop trying to give me a big head," she replied, coming out from behind the bar with her backpack.

"You have made quite the impression, young lassie. I seen all those men trying to give you their phone numbers. Doesn't it get hard declining them all?" Burt teased.

"I'd like to see who the lucky one might be that she says yes to. That will surely cause a fight or two," Jerome said and then sat down by the table.

Michaela took a seat. "Not going to happen. I don't date. It's not on my agenda right now."

"And what is, may I ask?" Jerome asked.

"My house, fixing it up, trying to make it into a home." She looked at Burt, he smiled.

"Which is why you need two friends like us to count on. So why not continue where you and I left off in the back room earlier. What's going on and how can we help?" Burt asked. She looked at Jerome, who stared at her intently.

"Burt, it's not that simple."

"Sure it is. You tell us what's going on and we help you to figure things out."

"There's nothing to figure out."

"Then why the secrecy, the police, the call in the back room, your resistance to talk about yourself, where you came from, your family?"

"I don't have any family. It doesn't matter where I came from because I'm here now. And I don't like to talk about myself."

"How do you do that?" Jerome asked.

"Do what?"

"Twist it back so we can't ask you the same questions again? Burt thinks you're in trouble. After twenty-five years on the force, I can tell that you're hiding something, so what gives?"

She threw up her hands in frustration. "Listen, I think that you're both really nice men. I like how you run this place, how you gave me a chance to work here, and how you're so willing to help a stranger. But I don't need any help. I don't need anything. I'm just trying to fit in, survive, and stay out of trouble."

"Then what's the trouble following you?" Burt asked her.

She sighed. She stared at Burt and Jerome. "I'm sorry, but I just can't talk about it."

"If there's going to be some trouble around here, we want to have your back and be prepared," Jerome stated.

She stood up, placed her backpack onto her shoulder. "I promise not to bring any trouble here. I'll be long gone before it even reaches this doorstep. Good night, guys. See you tomorrow." She headed toward the back door.

"You taking your bike home?" Jerome asked.

"Yep, it's the easiest form of transportation around here."

"We can give you a ride," Jerome told her.

"I'm fine. But thank you, again."

"Text me when you get home, so that I know you got there safely," Burt told her, and she chuckled.

"I will."

After she left, Burt looked at Jerome. "I hope there isn't someone trying to hurt her."

"You think so?"

"It sounded like something like that on her phone call. She did say that she would leave town if she had to."

"Leave town? What could be so bad that she would have to do that? Unless she's running from the law?"

"No way. If she were, she never would have stepped into that sheriff's department, nor would she react to Jake the way she does."

"You saw that, too? All three of them like her."

"What's not to like? Mary and I raised our sons well. They know a good woman when they see one."

Jerome raised his eyebrows at Burt.

"Oh hell, I know, but Lisa was bad news. I knew it and you knew it from the start. But my sons couldn't see past her bullshit. I still don't know how it all ended so badly, but whatever that woman did to them, it scarred them deeply."

"I know. And they haven't looked at another woman since."

"Until now. Until Smiley.

"Now wouldn't that be something else?" Burt smiled.

"It sure would be, but Michaela doesn't seem interested."

"Oh she is. She's just scared, and it probably has something to do with what she's keeping secret. Maybe my sons will get her to talk."

"Are you going to tell them about your concerns?"

"No need to. Jake seems like he's thinking similar thoughts. I'll just let it be, and who knows, maybe in a few months, I'll gain myself a daughter-in-law."

"That's a bit presumptuous of you."

"Hey, you've known me most of my life. How often have I been wrong when it comes to women?"

"Never."

"Thank you, sir. Now let's get the heck out of here. We gotta do this all over again tomorrow."

"Burt, it is tomorrow," Jerome teased and Burt chuckled.

Chapter 4

Joyce was at her desk in the sheriff's office going over some faxes that had come in. Joyce had already taken out the unimportant ones and handed over a stack of others. There were pictures of suspects wanted in various crimes around other states, and she would cross-check the information into the national computer system to see if the suspects had been caught, spotted anywhere, or could be in the vicinity of town. Treasure Town was nestled in between two major tourist areas on the shorelines. However, on both tips of the island were areas that only locals occupied.

Across a small bridge, always filled with traffic daily, with visitors coming and going between islands, there was a Marine Patrol base that secured and patrolled the area on water, maintained water safety, and also stood as a training facility for military personnel.

Joyce cross-checked the pictures and information she received through those databases as well. When she came up with one individual still wanted, she read the information. Seeing that the man was also wanted for questioning in a murder investigation by the FBI, she immediately brought it to the attention of the sheriff. Treasure Town was a safe place to live. Most people around here thought that had a lot to do with the sheriff and his deputies, as well as how on top of things they kept. Having so many military residents and a base nearby helped, too. No criminal murderer from New York was going to try and hide out here in Treasure Town. Not if Joyce had anything to do with it.

* * * *

Sheriff Jake McCurran sat at his desk and looked over the paperwork Joyce handed him earlier. He would be sure to get the picture of the guy out to his deputies.

As he finished going over some e-mails on his computer, his curiosity got the better of him as he searched the Internet for the video. He was pretty pissed off at whoever made a copy of the in-house surveillance footage. He gathered the deputies for a meeting and explained the ramifications to the department, never mind to Miss Smitt, who was after all, a victim in the whole incident.

As he came across multiple copies of the video, he clicked on the one with the most hits. He blinked his eyes and read the number a second time. Was that a million, six hundred and forty-two hits?

He ran his hand along his chin and shook his head. The damn Internet was a dangerous tool. An entrepreneur's gold mine and a predator's playground.

He hit play and watched the video unfold. It was upsetting to see how the stupid rookie deputy undid Leonard's handcuffs as Leonard pretended to speak nicely to the receptionist. It was obvious by Leonard's body language that he was under the influence. Jake felt pissed off all over again, and as he watched the entire video, he felt sick to his stomach seeing Leonard touch Michaela. It was nauseating, and really, he couldn't blame her for her reaction.

As he watched her manipulate the gun from Leonard's hand, twist his wrist, grab the gun, force him to the ground, knee him in the spine, and then hold the gun to his head, he was shocked at how quickly it all went down. He stared at her thighs, her skirt lifted to practically her waist as she straddled Leonard and held the gun like a professional officer of the law.

The woman looked gorgeous and capable. But she also looked well trained. Why would a young woman, with no professional need that he knew of, need training like that? He rubbed his chin as he stared at the video, her handing him the gun, him looking like a moron for not taking care of the situation and her storming away. No wonder everyone asked him if he was pissed off. She looked like Wonder Woman, and he looked like a bozo with his head up his ass.

He chuckled to himself. He actually wasn't pissed off. He was aroused. Holy fucking shit. No wonder the video took off as it had. Michaela looked sexy and capable. It was impressive. She was impressive.

As he thought about it, he realized that it also made him feel jealous. Other men were watching this video. Other men would go to The Station to see her, flirt with her. What if someone tried something? Then what?

His concern was overwhelming, and he glanced at the clock, saw it was nearly lunchtime.

He logged out of his computer and headed out of the office, telling Joyce that he had something to take care of and would be gone for lunch. He headed outside to the patrol truck knowing exactly what he needed to do. He needed to warn a certain little lady that trouble could come looking for her, and perhaps she needed a friend, after all.

* * * *

Michaela was trying to fix the stairs to the attic when she smelled the smoke. As she pulled the ladder down, half of it came off the hinges, making her scream and nearly fall. But the smoke was getting a bit heavier and she wasn't certain where it was coming from. Assuming that perhaps it had something to do with a faulty wire again, she didn't want to panic and call the fire department. As she climbed up, cutting her elbow on splitting wood in the frame of the attic, she saw the smoke coming from some kind of unit toward the front part of the house.

Of course it was an extremely hot day. She started coughing as the odd-smelling smoke filled her lungs. Noticing where the fire seemed to be coming from, she crawled closer just as some flames ignited.

Michaela screamed and then grabbed for whatever she could reach to try and put out the fire. She was coughing heavily now, but determined to not freak out, even though she thought she heard sirens in the distance. Perhaps one of the neighbors saw the smoke and called.

Michaela swung the large, dirty quilted blanket against the square box, as she pulled up her tank top to cover her mouth and nose. She was trying to not inhale too much of the stuff when she heard the crackling and a pop.

The deep sound of a fire truck's horn as well as sirens blaring penetrated through the walls of the home. She was relieved, but it seemed the fire that started was dissipating.

"Michaela?" She heard her name through the smoke and her coughing.

"Here!" she yelled out, crawling back toward the opening. She was coughing more and had to stop several times when she saw the firefighter appear by the square opening. She wondered how he or she got up there considering that the ladder was broken, but then she heard a bang and a gushing sound hit the window in the attic. She fell onto her side as water sprayed the window.

"I found someone," the firefighter yelled. She held the tank top against her mouth and nose as the firefighter came all the way up. Then there was another one.

"Michaela, what the hell are you doing up here?" one yelled and then coughed.

She saw his face, his eyes, as she crawled closer. Her heart raced. It was Hal, and the second firefighter was Billy.

"I think it's out," she yelled from under her shirt.

"Get over here. Bear, I'm going to hand her down to you. Then I'll check the situation."

Hal reached for her, lifting her in the small tight space as if she were a toy doll. Then he mumbled something she didn't understand as he lowered her to Bear's waiting arms. The men had call signs she totally understood why. Bear was as big as one, as he wrapped his arms around her and carried her away down the hallway. It was all clear in the house, just slightly hazy.

"You can put me down. I can walk," she said and then coughed.

"Are you crazy? You can die from smoke inhalation. You could have passed out up there," he reprimanded but didn't let her down. As they came outside, she saw the multiple fire trucks and realized in an instant how serious the fire was. A glance up as she continued coughing, and she saw the fire by the eves of the house, directly where the attic was and where wiring was sparking. As she followed the direction of the hanging wires, she saw it lead below to the front porch.

That was where she'd fixed the light that kept blinking last night. The front porch light wouldn't stay lit, and finally she changed the wires and added a new bulb. Obviously the entire wiring from the front porch to the attic needed to be redone.

"Goddamn it," she said and then coughed as Bear carried her to the fire truck. He set her down on the back and began checking her over. Placing a mask over her mouth and nose, he ordered her to take slow breaths. At first she coughed a few times and tried to remove the mask, but Bear kept one hand on her hip and upper thigh and one on the mask holding her, and it in place. She stared at his firm expression as she did what he told her to. His green eyes held hers and boy did he seem upset.

She absorbed the sight of him in front of her, the way it felt being carried from the attic and her home by him, and even how Hal had lowered her to Billy's arms so gently. Here she was filled with lustful thoughts as multiple firefighters put out the fire and checked for the cause and the damage.

"Jesus, is she okay? What the hell happened?"

She heard the sheriff's voice and immediately turned to look. There he was, fully dressed in uniform, and he looked concerned as well.

She took over holding the mask in place as Billy placed his hand on her shoulder and neck and gently massaged her skin. She felt the instant attraction to him. How manly he was, and how huge his hand felt against her skin. Her nipples hardened, her core tightened. She swallowed hard as she looked at him and he held her gaze. His expression was like no other she had ever seen. He looked powerful, sexy, and mostly hungry. That realization stirred something in her she didn't recognize at all.

* * * *

Bear looked at his brother as he arrived. He was so worried about Michaela, too. The moment the call came into the station house, Jake had texted that the house was Michaela's. Both Billy and Hal made sure to find her immediately. They were shocked to locate her in the attic directly where the fire was and trying to put it out with a blanket while inhaling all that dangerous smoke.

As the paramedics arrived, they took over caring for her. But he couldn't resist caressing her shoulder and neck as she held the mask in place. She appeared so delicate and feminine. He was instantly protective, and even more surprising was how possessive he felt. He fixed the strap of her tank top, pulling it back into position gently so no one else could see down the cup of her bra to her plump breast.

He eased his hand away and let the paramedic take care of her and check her vitals as he spoke with Jake.

"What the fuck happened?"

"Hal and I found her upstairs in the attic. That's where the fire started. She's lucky that it didn't spread faster. She was up there inhaling smoke and trying to put it out herself, I think."

Billy could tell that his brother was pissed off at the details. Jake walked over to Michaela as the paramedic handed her a bottle of water to drink.

"Are you out of your mind? If you see smoke, think there's a fire, you get the hell out and you call 911. You don't go up there and try to face it on your own. You could have passed out or even died from inhaling that smoke."

"I was just trying to save the house," she said, her voice all froggy and kind of sexy. She coughed and then took another slug of water.

"Your life is more important than the house, Michaela."

She went to step down off the truck and she teetered. Bear wrapped an arm around her waist and hoisted her close against his turnout coat.

She stared up into his eyes, and he smiled at her. "You need to take it easy. The combination of inhaling the smoke and then taking in some oxygen to help clear your lungs can make you feel off-balance."

"No kidding." She held on to his forearms. Billy smiled and helped her to sit back down.

"I don't want you to move from here. I'm going to see what the actual cause of the fire was and what Hal found out. You stay put. You hear me?" he reprimanded as he pointed at her. She nodded her head as she crossed her legs and leaned back. The full tank top she wore couldn't conceal her voluptuous body or the deep cleavage. She was absolutely adorable, and he couldn't wait to get to know her. Maybe this little incident would help to break the ice? He could only hope so. Bear walked away and Jake crossed his arms and stood closely in front of her.

* * * *

Jake stepped forward and placed his hands onto Michaela's shoulders. He bent lower so he could whisper.

"I was so worried when the call came over the radio about a fire at your address." He stared at her, and she swallowed hard. He removed one hand and gently clutched her chin before caressing her skin with his thumb.

"You have to be more careful, baby."

The way he called her baby was enough to give her palpitations. She stared up at him.

"Jake, I'm fine. I told you that I could take care of myself."

He shook his head.

"I don't want to hear that nonsense anymore. Around here, friends stick together. I care about you."

"What? How? You don't even know me," she said with attitude.

"I'm planning on rectifying that situation and so are my brothers. Now sit tight, and we'll give you the okay when it's safe to go back inside."

He released her shoulders and she stared at him as he walked away. Did he just hint that he and his brothers, Billy and Hal, were interested in her?

"Miss, I see that your elbow is bleeding. Let me clean that up for you." A paramedic interrupted her thoughts and she nodded, still speechless after what Jake just said, never mind did. She was attracted to the three of them, but she shouldn't be. Especially since she may not even be sticking around this town for that much longer. With thoughts of her situation and the danger she was in, came thoughts of why she couldn't act on her attraction to Jake or to his brothers.

Plus, that type of relationship had never even crossed her mind, not even in fantasy. A ménage? Three men and one woman?

I've never even had a boyfriend. One boyfriend. How the hell could I even consider three boyfriends?

At once. She felt sick to her stomach with a combination of fear and curiosity. Those men can't be serious. They must just like to have fun and be wild in bed. Each of them were so damn sexy, they probably had had dozens of women, maybe even more between the three of them. She'd had none. Zip. Not even a boyfriend. Too fearful of being tricked, cheated, or just plain used.

The walls I've put up are pretty damn solid. Three sexy firefighters who like to share their women will not break those walls down. I've been hurt and heartbroken enough in my life. Nope, I'm not going to weaken now. I can't.

It was easier to remain alone and secluded than it was to open herself up for more pain, and more than likely more disappointment. Everyone in her life disappointed and failed her. A ménage relationship was just asking for it to fail and for them to break her heart and leave her as hollow as she felt right now.

"Excuse me, Michaela?" She turned toward an older man who joined her and the paramedic. She recognized him immediately. He lived next door, at the closest house to hers in the cul-de-sac.

"Yes."

He smiled. "I'm so glad that you're okay, and so is the house. When I saw the smoke and knew you were inside, I called the fire department right away. My name is Ike. Ike Mason." He introduced himself and held out his hand for her to shake.

She reached over with her right hand since the paramedic was wrapping her left. Ike chuckled but gently took her right hand.

"Michaela Smitt. It's nice to meet you, Ike, and thank you for calling in for help."

"No problem. I was so happy to see someone had brought the old Fennigan home. I'd hate for something like this to scare you off."

"Oh, no worries there. I don't scare too easily," she told him and then thought about how she might have to leave on a moment's notice if that hit man or Solomon came looking for her. She turned away and back toward her house which wasn't in terrible shape at all.

"It could have been a lot worse. Looks like you probably stopped that electrical fire from getting out of control." Hal interrupted her thoughts as he, Billy, Jake, and the fire chief came over.

"Michaela, this is Chief Martelli."

She smiled at the man as he shook her hand.

"How are you feeling, honey?" he asked her with a smile.

"I'm okay."

"Good to hear. The men were worried," he said, glancing at Billy and Hal.

Hal took position next to her.

"What caused it, do you know?" She asked.

"It appears to have been electrical. Something wired up through the eaves of the house from the outside. Not done by code at all."

"Great. Well, I can tell you it probably had something to do with the porch light. It kept flickering on and off since I bought the house. I changed the outlet and the bulb. It was working fine."

"Are you certain you knew what you were doing?" Hal asked.

She gave him the once-over. "Oh, I know what I'm doing. I don't mess around with the heavy electrical work, the minor stuff I can handle."

The chief cleared his throat.

"More than likely the problem wasn't in the outlet where the main connector was. It seems that the previous owner rigged his own source of wiring from up in the attic. Probably to hide it from an inspector. The faulty wire behind the walls of the siding finally gave out, and when they shorted, they caught fire by the small box up in the attic," the chief stated.

"It didn't help that the box was made out of wood, and there were old cardboard boxes and rags near it. I even found paint containers. It could have been worse. It could have blown up with you up there," Hal stated and then leaned his hand against the back of the fire truck right above her shoulder.

His turnout coat was undone, his gloves off, and she could see his bulging muscles beneath the tight blue T-shirt he wore. The man was flammable himself. Her heart raced as she held his gaze.

"You probably helped to stop the fire from getting out of control. Although I don't condone what you did. But you're safe, and the house is intact. You'll just need to get rid of all the junk up there in the attic," the chief continued.

"And you'll need an electrician to come in and check out all the wiring, so this can't happen anywhere else in the house," Jake added with his arms crossed in front of his chest. She felt like a child being reprimanded.

"Listen, I appreciate all the great advice. I'll be sure to go over everything more thoroughly tomorrow. I'm planning on gutting most of the place room by room, which means down to the beams beneath the sheet rock."

"My nephew works for an electrician. He's really good. I can have him come over here tomorrow and go through things with you," Ike offered.

"That's very nice of you. I'll let you know, Ike."

"Hey, I know the company his nephew works for. It's a good company and the owner is a friend of mine. I think that's a great idea, Ike," Jake added.

"Listen." She raised her voice and they all stared at her.

Michaela took a deep breath and then released it. "Listen, I appreciate the offers, but I can handle this on my own. Now, can I go inside to see the damage?"

"You may want to rest for the night, maybe take this on tomorrow. You did inhale a lot of smoke," Hal said as he placed his hand on her shoulder stopping her. He glided his hand down her arm, giving her goose bumps and making her shiver from the level of attraction she was feeling. He was sexy and very good looking. He gently turned her arm to look at the bandage.

"I'm fine, Hal. I just cut it on the flooring when the attic ladder fell." She pulled it from him and slowly eased between him and Billy to walk into her house. She would have run if she weren't trying so hard to prove her independence and desire to be left alone, and not let on to the dizziness she felt. She thanked the other firefighters as they cleaned up their equipment.

As she inhaled the smell of smoke in her home she wondered how she would even sleep tonight. *With no lights on, of course. God knows what else might catch on fire in this place.*

She looked at the mess in the hallway from where the attic stairs were lying on the ground. She leaned her head against the wall and closed her eyes.

Will I ever have peace in my life? Will there ever be a happy time, even a moment of normalcy and accomplishment? Or will my life eternally be filled with heartache, struggles, and fear?

She wiped away the tear she wouldn't let fall and pushed away from the wall. It was time to do what she always did when shit happened. She cleaned it up because no one else was going to help her to do it.

I'm alone in this godforsaken world. I know that, so why am I feeling ready to cry and just give up? Suck it up, Michaela. Like always.

* * * *

Michaela was startled as she heard the banging on the front door. It was seven o'clock in the morning on a Sunday. Who could be here? She hadn't even made coffee yet. She had gotten dressed in shorts and a tank top. It wasn't as hot as yesterday but she would be sweating soon enough. She had the mess from the fire to clean up before she could even think about moving on to the demolition work.

She looked at the front window as she made her way toward the front door, and her heart caught in her throat. She could see multiple trucks and guys carrying things from their vehicles. She opened the front door and there stood Jake with a large brown bag and a huge takeout container of coffee.

"Good morning, darling. Hope you didn't have breakfast yet. The chief's daughter sent all this stuff over from Sullivan's restaurant." He walked right by her and headed toward the kitchen. Hal was behind him along with Billy. They were carrying tools and some sort of square vacuum thing. A glance past them and she saw the electricians truck, Ike from next door, and about five other men.

"What are you doing here? What's all of this?" she asked, feeling her throat clog up with emotion.

Hal walked by her. "We're here to help. That's the kind of people who live in Treasure Town. When one of us is in trouble or needs some help, the community is there to pitch in. Sometimes you just need a friend or friends to help get through things." He set the machine thing down in the hallway.

"Let's grab some bagels and coffee and then get started in the attic. Lou is bringing by the other Dumpster," Jake told them. Michaela covered her mouth in awe as the other men came inside, introduced themselves, and then grabbed some bagels and coffee in her kitchen.

She walked into the hallway a moment and gathered her emotions. She'd never experienced anything like this before. No one cared about her. She was alone in this world. She didn't even know that people like this existed.

The arm wrapped around her waist from behind. She tried to step out of the hold but Jake held firmly and whispered against her hair.

"It's okay. You don't have to say a thing. It's no big deal, baby. Everyone heard about the fire, and about the problems with the house, and they wanted to pitch in and help you. You don't need to handle this alone. We're here."

"But I...I don't know what to say. I've never experienced anything like this before." She turned around. He held her still, and she leaned against the wall in the hallway. Jake reached down and caressed her cheek with the back of his hand.

"You're strong and you're brave, but everyone needs a little help now and then. Come have some coffee and bagels and then we'll get started."

She shook her head in disbelief at the offer and the generosity. "Thank you, Jake."

He smiled at her and then took her hand and led her back into the kitchen.

* * * *

Billy was working side by side with Michaela in the attic. They had passed down numerous items, clearing the entire attic of debris. Jake was installing the new attic stairs pull-cord along with Hal.

Billy watched Michaela struggling with the insulation. She was trying to tear it back in order to assist the electrician downstairs with locating another main line. She was tugging on the wire but it wasn't budging. Billy crawled along next to her, his body brushing against hers as he approached.

"Let me try," he whispered. Their gazes locked and he felt his heart pounding in his chest. All day he and his brothers took turns working by her. He didn't know if Hal and Jake took the opportunities that he did to rub against her, lock gazes with her, or absorb her natural beauty and strength. But right now, with gazes locked as he reached under the insulation and tugged the wire free, she mesmerized him.

So did the smudge of dust or dirt by her lower lip. Hell, the tiny droplets of perspiration dripping between her breasts aroused him, too. It brought some pretty wild images of her in bed with him and his brothers making love to her multiple times. They'd have her sedated and well loved in no time.

They heard the electrician yell from below that he got the wire. Michaela didn't move, nor did Billy.

He reached up and gently ran his thumb along her lower lip and the slight bit of dust.

She parted her lips and looked too damn sexy to not kiss. Leaning closer, he held her gaze, staring into her deep blue eyes as he whispered. "There was something on your lip."

"Oh," she replied and began to lower her head, but he moved his fingers to her chin, gripped it, and covered her lips with his.

The kiss started out slowly. Hell, he was only going to take a sample taste, but his desire and the attraction between them was too much and that kiss grew wild quickly. He wasn't sure how it happened, but he wound up halfway on top of her, felt her fingers running through his hair, pulling him closer as their tongues dueled for control of the kiss. She moaned into his mouth and he absorbed everything he could about the moment. The sweet taste of her, the scent of her perfume, and the burned wood left over from the fire. The humidity of the attic, their bodies perspiring, her breasts full and plump against his chest, and the feel of her petite body beneath his thighs and hips.

He ran his hand along her waist, past her ribs to cup her breast, and she lifted her thigh and tried to maneuver. They were losing breath from kissing so deeply, so wildly, and when he moved his mouth off her lips to her neck, he heard her rapid breathing. It matched his own.

"Billy. Billy we have to stop." She panted and he stopped kissing her to look down at her face. He saw the arousal and brightness in her eyes but also something else. His heart ached. His chest tightened. Did she not feel what he felt? *Oh God, please let her have felt the desire, the intensity like I did. I never felt like this before.*

"Stop?" he questioned, and now she looked like she was in pain.

"There's something sticking into my spine." She cringed.

"Oh shit." He slid to the side bringing her up and off her back. She half straddled him as she reached back and patted away at her shirt in the back.

"What is it?"

"I don't know but it is stinging."

He grabbed the flashlight as she turned on her knees. He gently lifted her top in the back noticing the shredded bits of wood. As he stared at her skin, he saw the splinter.

"Shit, you got a splinter on your back."

"Ouch. Can you pull it out?"

"Uhm, what exactly is going on up here?" Jake asked, staring at them from the top of the ladder.

He could only imagine what his brother was thinking with Billy holding Michaela's shirt up in the back.

"Splinter," he stated.

Jake's eyebrows crunched up.

"Come over here. I'm great at taking out splinters," he told her.

Michaela looked at Billy.

"Old attics, huh?" She pulled her bottom lip between her teeth and he reached out and ran his thumb along it.

"I'll never look at old attics the same way again, baby, thanks to you."

She turned a nice shade of red as she lowered her eyes and crawled toward Jake. Billy winked at his brother, and saw the look in his eyes. Jake would get out the splinter, and then he would take a taste of Michaela for himself.

* * * *

Michaela almost felt dizzy with giddiness. It was so silly, stupid actually, to react to a kiss in such a way, yet every ounce of her reacted. She was so inexperienced in many ways. For one, in the sex department.

She was a twenty-four-year-old virgin. And why? Because of the fear she had of giving away any part of her whatsoever because of her family. Her mother failed her, her father failed her and abandoned her, and even her sister, who she took a shot to the heart for, failed her. Even in the final moments before Annette's death, her sister still supported Solomon, her boyfriend. She didn't even look at Michaela.

In fact, when Michaela showed up, her sister asked why she was there. She told Michaela to leave, and that she didn't have a sister. There was never any love or connection at all.

It broke Michaela's heart because she had made the trip to New York in hopes of salvaging the only family she had left, her only blood relative, and that was the response she had gotten. It took Michaela some time to realize that giving any part of her to anyone one else might never happen. She just wouldn't be able to handle that type of pain and disappointment again.

As Jake took her hand and guided her toward the bathroom with Hal right in the hallway, she focused on trying not to pass out or overanalyze the kiss with Billy.

But Jake closed the door slightly to the small old bathroom and told her to take off the tank top.

"What?"

"I need to see the splinter and make sure there aren't more."

She swallowed hard as he opened the medicine cabinet and rummaged through it.

"The tweezers are in there and I can grab a needle in the basket of sewing supplies under the sink." She bent down and the splinter ached on her spine.

"Let me," he scolded. She stood up straight and watched the oversized sheriff look for what he needed, including some peroxide and cotton balls.

He stood up and told her to turn around to face the mirror and vanity.

His lips were next to her shoulder. "Relax and let me take care of you."

She closed her eyes and imagined how incredible life could be if he was sincere in that statement and she were willing to give it a try. What would it be like to be cared for by Jake? By Hal and even Billy?

Oh God, I like them. I'm so attracted to them. I basically kissed Billy and ran my hands over his body possessively. Oh Lordy, this is insane.

"I need this tank top off, honey. You have more than one splinter."

When his large hands landed on her hips from behind, she thought she might burst out a moan. He was big. His hands, his body, his chest, arms, every ounce of him was large and muscular. She took a deep breath as he began lifting her tank top up and over her head.

She grabbed it from his hands and placed it over her breasts where the bra barely covered her, and to hide the scar from her bullet wound. All she needed was for the sheriff to see *that*. She was a bit embarrassed by her choice of the purple, sexy, lace bra she wore, but bras and panties were her one obsession. She loved all colors, all styles of skimpy thongs, lacy, satin, you name it and she had a matching set.

He trailed his fingers along her skin and she swallowed hard.

"How bad? Can you get them out?" she asked, looking at him through the reflection in the mirror. His eyes were focused on her back.

She felt his warm breath caress along her skin.

"I think so. I don't want to hurt you." He reached for the tweezers first. His other hand remained on her hip, and she felt the warmth, the masculinity of his hold. Every feminine part of her reacted. Her pussy clenched, her breasts felt full, and her nipples hardened instinctually.

"It's okay. Just do it so we can get back to help the others," she whispered.

He stared at her through the reflection in the mirror and then looked back down at her back. She felt him begin to pinch around where the splinter was. He mumbled a few times under his breath and carefully pulled the first one out. He showed her the splinter and she made a funny face. It was bigger than she thought it would be.

"Two more to go," he told her, rinsing the tweezers and brushing his forearm against her breast as he reached under her arms.

She felt his hips against her ass, and she found herself slightly bending over the sink and counter, imagining what it would be like to be fucked from behind by Jake.

His hand squeezed her hip, and he thrust gently against her but quickly pulled back, making her wonder if she imagined it. Her pussy clenched and she closed her eyes as he pulled the other two splinters out. He poured peroxide on the cotton balls and cleaned up her skin.

"That should do it." He ran his palm along her back. She was shocked yet accepting when his arm wrapped around her midsection from behind and pulled her back against him.

She gasped as they locked gazes through the mirror.

"You're a gorgeous woman. You have beautiful skin, and I am so aroused right now, baby. Just thinking about you rolling around upstairs in the attic with Billy has me wanting to do a lot of things to you and this body."

"Things?" she whispered, and he bent her forward slightly as he held her around the waist and kissed along her neck.

"Lots of wild, crazy things." He suckled her neck in a sensitive spot as he eased his jean-covered cock against her ass. She felt her pussy cream and nearly moaned aloud.

"Jake."

"Shhh. Not a word. No denials. Not now when I've got you in my arms and am about to kiss you. That's something I've been wanting to do since I met you."

He reached up and gently turned her face toward him while remaining against her back.

He rubbed his thumb along her lower lip and she stared up into his blue eyes.

"Ah hell." He pressed his lips against hers. She accepted his kiss and his tongue as he plunged it between her teeth and she turned in his arms.

He lifted her up. She wrapped her arms best she could up and around his shoulders as he continued to kiss her deeply. His hands were everywhere. On her waist, up her ribs to her breasts as he thrust his hips gently against her. She thrust back, feeling incredibly aroused and filled with desire. She'd never experienced these type of strong, combustible emotions. Not ever.

She ran her hands through his crew cut hair, and when he pinched her nipple, she moaned into his mouth.

They kept kissing until they both couldn't catch their breath and he eased his mouth along her neck and collarbone. Michaela tilted her head back as he continued to use his mouth to explore her. His mouth went lower. She gripped his shoulders, never feeling so feminine and desirable and damn sexy. She was panting for air. He was pressing her bra down and licking across her nipple when he stopped. It was sudden, and she was so lost in the desire, she felt she wanted to demand for him to continue.

"What is this?" he asked, shoving her immediately back into the real world, back into her fucked-up past and life.

She looked down to where the scar from the gunshot wound was.

She shoved down and away from him, or at least tried to, but he lifted her up into his arms and pressed her against the wall. Instinctively she wrapped her legs around his waist but kept her eyes closed and her face turned.

"Look at me. Fucking look at me right now, Michaela."

His firm, authoritative voice had her tilting her head back against the wall before she looked at him.

"This is a gunshot wound."

"Please, Jake. Please don't ask me questions."

"Fuck that," he barked at her and squeezed her tighter, grinding his teeth.

"After the kiss we just shared, the chemistry between us, and you think I'll let you push me away?"

She felt her emotions getting the better of her. That kiss, his touch, Billy's touch and kiss, was all so arousing and mind blowing. She wondered instantly what it would feel like when Hal kissed her. And she knew he would. Hell, these brothers came as a package. It was inevitable.

She swallowed hard. She had to stop this conversation from happening.

"Not now, Jake. Everyone is here working. Not now. I'm not ready."

He stared at her. His blue eyes were filled with so much emotion. Did he think she was a criminal? Did he really care for her or was this just lust, curiosity, or interest in the new woman in town? Crazy thoughts were going through her mind about whether or not she could trust him and his brothers. After just two lethal kisses and here she was debating about baring her soul to them.

Then Jake lowered his mouth to her chest and pressed his lips gently against the scar.

A tear escaped from her eye. There was no stopping it. This man, these men, in the last twenty-four hours had shown her more compassion and empathy than she'd ever experienced in all of her twenty-four years of life.

She reached up and ran her fingers along his hair and then placed her palm against his cheek as he lifted his lips up and stared at her.

"Are you for real?" she whispered.

"This is real," he replied, letting his other hand cup her ass as he pressed his thick, hard cock against her crotch. Despite the layer of clothing between them, she felt the heat, the hardness, and the desire.

"These emotions, this attraction between all of us, is most definitely real, Michaela. I want to know everything about you. I want to share everything about me with you, but mostly, I want to earn your trust, make you look at me and my brothers and know that we can protect you, be honest with you, and maybe even love you."

His mention of love shocked her. She shook her head and pushed and wiggled from his arms.

He allowed her to step down, and pull her tank top into position.

"Michaela." He grabbed her hand and pulled it up and against his chest. They locked gazes.

"Friends first," he told her as they heard their names being called by Hal.

Friends first? Is he out of his mind? The last type of relationship on my mind after that is to be friends. I'm in a bit of a situation here. What am I going to do? How am I going to explain things to them?

* * * *

Hal was helping Michaela set up the machines that would help pull the smoky smell from the house despite the fact that they replaced all the walls where the fire was. The electrician and Ike rewired all the main wiring around the house that had been altered by the previous homeowner. It appeared that most of the house had its original wiring or new wiring done by a licensed electrician and to code. That gave Hal and his brothers as well as Michaela some relief.

With everyone's help they had been able to tear down the Sheetrock and replace it with better insulation and new Sheetrock. They knocked down the wall in the kitchen as Michaela had wanted, and they helped demolition everything and leave a clean start for the rest of her construction.

He was impressed with her knowledge of construction and building work, and also the fact that she wanted to salvage the older qualities of the home, restore it to its original design in some aspects, starting with ridding the place of all the carpeting and allowing the hardwood floors to show. She had lots of plans and great ideas, as she showed him a picture of the kitchen she wanted to do.

They were both leaning over the table looking at the designs as she pointed around the room showing him where everything would go. Their arms rubbed against one another and he stopped looking at the design to absorb her beauty. She was sweet, strong, and stunning. She didn't mind getting dirty or breaking a nail, and she didn't back down from challenges, instead seemed to take those challenges on with determination and strength.

Even as the electrician's friend, a builder, told her about the process of restoring the original staircase, she just nodded her head, appeared determined, and said thank you for the information. He caught the guys watching her as well and had to set them straight about him and his brothers' interest. Word would spread fast that the McCurran brothers were staking a claim to Michaela. Now they would have to convince her to let her guard down and let them in.

She stood up and smiled at him. "What do you think?" she asked, still focused on her designs and what she just told him, but he was too absorbed in watching her and the need to kiss her.

He reached up and placed his hand against her cheek. "I think that you're amazing. I love the designs and your determination to restore a lot of the great character of this house to its original form."

She smiled as she placed her hand on his waist and began to say thank you. He took her touching him and leaning forward as an invite to kiss her. Moving his hand under her hair to the base of her head, he leaned down and kissed her.

That kiss grew deeper and deeper as he lifted her up by her ass and placed her on the last counter that remained in the room. It shook slightly but he had a good hold on her. That possessive feeling and need to protect her and watch over her was so strong. Their tongues collided as they dueled for control of the kiss until he cupped both her cheeks in his palms and took complete control.

Easing his mouth from hers, he locked gazes with her and smiled.

"You're one sexy woman, Michaela. I could kiss you all day long."

"But you can't. You need to share."

Both of them turned to see Jake and Billy standing in the doorway smiling.

She lowered her face to Hal's chest as he chuckled and wrapped her in his arms. A place he hoped she would be more often from here on out.

* * * *

Michaela had thanked everyone for their help as they left the neighborhood.

She headed inside and sat down on the back porch as Hal called her to come on out. It was a beautiful night, the sun was setting, and she was exhausted.

Billy handed her a beer, and Jake was already occupying one of the other seats, leaving her an empty seat between him and Billy.

Billy patted the cushion. "Take a load off, Smiley."

She shook her head, took a slug of beer, and plopped down onto the chair. The moment she did she felt her muscles sigh in relief from taking a break from all the hard work.

"Achy?" Jake asked, watching her.

She nodded her head. "I'm going to be out cold the moment my head hits the pillow." She opened her eyes to find all three men watching her. "What?" she asked.

"You're amazing. Do you know that?" Billy asked her.

She shook her head. "Stop. I'm just determined to get this house in great shape."

"What made you decide to buy this house in its condition?" Hal asked, eyeing her over with that sexy expression that came so naturally to the man. She understood why his call sign was Hollywood. Hal could definitely pass as a movie star.

"It was cheap," she replied. Then she chuckled. "I'm just kidding. I was visiting to see if this was a town, a place I would like to live, when I came across this neighborhood. The other houses are so nice, and well kept. This house looked abandoned, like someone gave up on it. I guess I wanted to give it another chance. You know, bring back the life that was once inside and outside of the home. You guys saw all the beautiful woodwork throughout. Can you believe that someone covered up those high windows with the stained glass at the top? You can't even buy that kind of history and style. And the railing, the staircase? God, that is going to be so freaking gorgeous when it's done."

"Honey, you've got such vision. And I tell you, I thought you were nuts to buy this house, but seeing it through your ideas and through your eyes, I'm excited to see what you do with it," Billy told her.

She smiled. "Thank you. And thank you so very much for today. I was feeling kind of down and defeated after the fire yesterday. I was afraid to turn on any lights last night so I slept with a flashlight on in the bedroom." She chuckled and then took another slug of beer.

"You should have called us, baby. We would have come over here to keep you safe and warm," Hal said and winked.

She stared at him. "Please don't tell me that women fall for lines like that?"

Hal and Jake laughed.

"That wasn't a line. I would have come over here in a flash if you needed me just to keep you company. God knows I couldn't sleep a wink last night worried about you in this house and what else could go wrong."

His sincerity was so apparent she couldn't believe the heaviness in her heart.

"That's really sweet," she replied.

"Nothing would have happened except for what you wanted to happen between us," Hal added.

She lowered her eyes and held the beer can.

"About that. About today," she began to say.

Billy covered her hand.

She locked gazes with him.

"Don't. Don't even try to deny the attraction between the four of us, and how powerful it is. Don't push us away for whatever reason you feel it's necessary to."

"We wouldn't hurt you, Michaela. We're good men. We've been hurt before and know it's a shitty thing to do. You can trust us," Hal added.

She stood up and walked over toward the railing where Jake was but a bit away from him.

"Trust, well to be honest with you all, trust just doesn't come easy for me."

"Why?" Billy asked.

She looked at him. "For a lot of reasons. Reasons I'm just not ready to share with three men I hardly know."

"Get to know us then. Hell, baby, you can't deny how good it was to kiss and to touch," Billy said.

"Oh, I'm not denying it, Billy. Remember I have the marks on my back from the splinters that Jake needed to remove from the impact of your kisses."

They all chuckled.

Billy grabbed her hand and pulled her closer and between his legs. "Sweetheart, I promise to kiss you lying down like that on a hell of a lot softer and safer surface than the upstairs attic floor."

She chuckled as she squeezed his shoulders, and he caressed the sides of her thighs and then back of her thighs until both hands inched under her shorts and cupped her ass.

"Billy."

She twisted out of his hold and turned around only for him to pull her onto his lap. His hold was snug, and she leaned back and enjoyed being cradled in Billy's arms.

"Honesty is important in a relationship, Michaela. We have reservations, too," he told her, and she sensed the concern in his tone.

Had someone hurt them before? Did they try this ménage relationship and it went all wrong? That gave her more anxiety, but then she felt jealous and concerned. What woman had gained their interest, had shared their bed, perhaps even their hearts? She gulped.

"You don't need to tell me about the other women you have shared. I don't think I want to know," she said with a bit of attitude.

"Michaela, it's a personal decision and choice a lot of people make. We have many friends, retired military and other professions that chose a ménage relationship for personal reasons. We can tell you exactly why we want this type of relationship," Jake said.

"I want to know why. I want to understand it. But it sounds like you've tried it with another women and it failed."

"It failed for lots of reasons," Billy said and then squeezed her against him. She turned sideways on his lap and looked at him.

"Like what reasons?"

They were silent and it made her feel bad for prying, but yet, she wanted to understand why they wanted to share one woman between them when they were each so good looking, so kind and generous. They were older, a lot older, and more mature than her.

"Lots of reasons, Michaela. Things we still can't talk about, because it still hurts," Hal added.

She swallowed hard. "I can understand that."

"You seem like you can. I get the feeling that you've been hurt before, too. Is that what makes you afraid to give this relationship a try?" Jake asked her.

"Jake, I know nothing about this type of relationship, about, well let's just say about a lot of things." She nibbled her lip. She couldn't exactly tell them she was a virgin, and she also couldn't tell them about her trust issues and fear of abandonment. Hell, she was fighting those demons herself for too many years now. It was easier to just keep fighting and hiding. These men couldn't change that. Could they?

"I think you know more than you think. I also believe that you're very strong-willed, determined to achieve the goals you set out to achieve. You're independent, probably to a fault."

"To a fault?" she asked, feeling insulted.

"I do believe Hal and I found you in the attic at the source of the fire where you could have gotten seriously hurt," Billy stated.

"Oh, and in my office with a gun to your head, you decided that you needed to take matters into your own hands when you disarmed the gunman holding you hostage because of your lack of patience with my handling of the situation," Jake said with his arms crossed in front of his chest.

"Hey, that guy was molesting me in front of you and all those deputies. A woman has to have her limitations."

"You could have gotten hurt," he replied.

"It was a chance I was willing to take, Jake."

"Well this type of relationship isn't exactly like staring down a barrel of a gun, sweetheart, but it does involve a commitment, total honesty and exclusivity," Hal told her.

If only they knew about the barrel of a gun and how true that was.

"Tell me why you want this."

"My brothers and I are close. The only time we were apart was during our time serving our country. We weren't stationed together but it didn't lessen our connection and bond," Jake told her.

"It's like we felt whole and complete, but also secure with our brothers. We're a team, and the trust we have is deeper and more genuine than with anyone else," Hal added.

Billy caressed his palm under her tank top and over her belly.

"Our friends shared their experiences with us, and their fears as well. We've seen some heavy shit in the service, on the force, and in the fire department. Things that could trigger some past experiences or make us react in a way we might need our brothers in support for. We realized pretty quickly that we all want a woman, a wife, someone to share and start a family with. We've seen other successful ménage relationships, and we know they are real and concrete. We want that, too."

"But what about jealousy? What about growing bored of the same woman or wanting or needing her at the same time but maybe she's not able to provide for more than one man simultaneously?" Michaela asked. Her head was beginning to hurt from thinking about all the things that could go wrong.

"You could handle it. We've never felt this close, this attracted to a woman, at the same time like we do with you," Hal stated.

Billy kissed along her neck and then moved his hand up and cupped her breast.

He blew warm breath against her ear, making her shiver.

"Right now, how do you feel, Michaela?" Jake asked.

She locked gazes with him as Billy continued to massage her breast. She could see the hunger in Jake's eyes, and she knew if she turned to look at Hal, his eyes would reveal the same thing.

Billy ran the palm of his other hand along her inner thigh and up to the V between her legs. She shivered again, but wiggled her ass, feeling Billy's cock grow harder and thicker under her ass and back.

"How do you feel?" Hal asked her, getting down off the chair and kneeling on the floor next to the chair she and Billy were in.

"Nervous."

"No, not nervous, but aroused, excited, curious, and comfortable," Jake whispered.

"Comfortable?" she asked but then closed her eyes and moaned as Billy pinched her nipple under her shirt and bra while he rubbed his other palm up and down the V between her thighs.

"Three men are with you right now. Hal and I are watching our brother, Billy, bringing you pleasure, and we want so badly to join in and make you moan from our touches, too. But we're trying to go slow. We want you to feel safe, comfortable, and accepting to each of our touches," Jake said.

Hal reached over and cupped her chin. "How turned on are you right now, knowing that we're watching our brother massage your breast and pinch your nipple all while he rubs that sweet little cunt?"

"Oh God." She moaned and felt the tiny spasms of cream release from her pussy.

"That's right. You know this is real. This isn't a game, a fetish, a one-time thing," Hal added.

Hal leaned forward and licked the seam of her lips before plunging his tongue into her mouth. She immediately grabbed onto his head and kissed him back.

She felt Jake move between her legs and undo the zipper on her shorts as she struggled with allowing them this intimacy and seeing where it led, or stopping them.

When she felt Jake's lips softly press against her thighs, she moaned into Hal's mouth. Jake made good use of his fingers by pulling off her shorts.

"That's it, Michaela. Feel the three of us touching you. Embrace the sensations. Feel comfortable and safe with us," Billy whispered against her bare shoulder. As soon as she felt the difference in temperature with her shorts off and then Jake's kisses moving between her inner thighs, she started to feel overwhelmed.

Billy cupped her other breast as he pinched one nipple. Hal stroked his tongue deeper into her mouth as he held a fistful of her hair so dominantly and controlling it awoke some primal need inside of her. Feeling the three amazing men attack her in such a primal way, and that was exactly what it was, an attack. On her heart, her body, her flesh, and her soul. She never felt such deep emotions from touches, and kisses alone. This was an intimacy she knew nothing about. It was a case of emotional overload as she fought between giving in to the sensations or running for her life. It was easier to not feel anything, and have a hollow heart, than to feel like this. She felt desirable, she was safe and sexy, and she felt on the verge of losing herself.

Jake pushed aside her panties and stroked his thumbs along her pussy lips.

"Oh," she moaned as she pulled from Hal's mouth.

"Easy, darling. Nice and easy, just relax."

"I can't. I've never. Oh God, I can't." She moaned as Jake thrust a finger up into her cunt and her body exploded.

* * * *

Michaela shot up off of Billy's lap and nearly stumbled. Jake was there to steady her by her hips, and she looked so fucking incredible and sexy, Billy reached for her.

"Oh God, Michaela, you should see what you look like," Billy whispered.

She was panting, and trying to step back into her shorts. Her breasts were pouring from the cups of her bra, her thong panties hung revealing a smooth pink mound that made his lips water. But then he spotted the shadow on her chest. The one above her breast on the left side.

He pulled her to him.

"What is this?" He pressed the strap lower and stared at the scar. "A gunshot wound?" His eyes must have appeared as if they were popping out of his head.

Then he heard Hal. "You were shot?"

She pulled away, fixed the strap of her bra and the tank top, and then rezipped her shorts.

"Please go. Please leave," she stated, turning around and holding herself.

"Absolutely not," Jake said in that determined, bossy tone of his as he lifted Michaela up into his arms and carried her into the house. Billy looked at Hal.

"She was shot. That is definitely a gunshot wound," Billy said as he stood up.

"I'm getting a bad feeling here, bro. I'm thinking some crazy shit."

"We'll find out the truth. We know how to handle things this time, Hal. Trust is earned, and if we're going to continue a relationship with Michaela, our lust, our desire to make love to her can't outweigh the greater need of trust. We know all too well how badly betrayal hurts. Let's go."

* * * *

"Put me down, Jake."

"I will. In your bed."

"No, Jake. I'm not having sex with the three of you."

"Not tonight, but you will be ours. I can guarantee it."

"Oh yeah, how? What are you going to do, force me?" she asked, and he lowered her onto the bed.

"Of course not. But you see, darling, I got this little thing called gut instinct. I'm a law enforcement officer. It means I have a great sense about people." His brothers walked in and they stood behind him.

"And what are your instincts telling you?" she asked him, half not wanting to have this conversation. She was already in emotional overload. Despite the fear of telling them the truth and her story, she was still aroused, her pussy was still wet, and now all three large men were practically suffocating the last ounce of her resolve by taking up every inch of space in her bedroom. They were too sexy, too filled with muscles, attitude, and sex appeal to turn away and deny. They were a lethal force, and she was weak to their spell of appeal.

"You like to keep to yourself. You don't share any personal information about yourself. You panicked over the release of the video from the department to the Internet, and you immediately made a phone call after I told you about the video. You have a scar that indicates you were shot, and by the looks of it, within the last year.

The way you talked about the house looking abandoned and unloved made me feel like you were talking about yourself, and your need to be loved and cared for. You think you're all alone, and maybe you have been, but that's going to change."

She closed her eyes and shook her head in denial. How could he be so perceptive?

She drew her knees up to her chest and rested her chin on her knees.

"I think you should go. I'm tired. I need a shower, and my head hurts."

He reached out and caressed her hair. Was it supposed to be fatherly, or like a caregiver's caress to the emotionally distraught child? She knew that wasn't the case, but her defense mechanisms went up so easily, and she wanted to resist the effects Jake's caress alone provided at the moment.

"It's going to be okay. I can spare a bit more patience for you."

She lifted her head up and stared at him and then his brothers then back to him again.

"I don't need a father figure, never mind three in my life," she snapped. When she went to get up, he gripped her tank top and pressed his hand over her waist, causing her to fall to her back and against the pillow.

He leaned over her, and looking into his blue eyes, all she could think about were his lips against hers, his fingers stroking her needy, inexperienced cunt, and getting lost in his embrace as well as in Billy's and Hal's. They totally changed her outlook on ménage, and all it had to offer a lost soul like herself.

"Baby, the last thing I intend to do is come off as fatherly. In fact, if it weren't for the fact that we're all exhausted and I know that you need time, I would have had you stripped naked by now and my cock deep inside you."

She parted her lips, nearly moaning from his words. He stroked his finger along her lips and jaw as he held her gaze.

"Trust is earned. We're going to start working on that. All of us, immediately." He leaned down and kissed her softly, and on instinct, or just her own emotional and physical reaction, she hugged him to her.

"I need time. Please, Jake. I just need time."

Chapter 5

Jake pulled the sheriff's truck into Michaela's driveway. Between his schedule and his brothers', they had been stopping by to spend time with her and to make her feel more comfortable. After speaking with Hal and Billy, both men were concerned over Michaela's experiences, and her possible inability to open up her heart to them. It seemed to him that Michaela hadn't received the love she should have had as a child and young adult.

In an attempt to save a part of the family, she went to see her sister and wound up in a heap of trouble. She didn't even talk about the fact that she saw her sister get shot and killed. She didn't even get into the lengthy recovery process from her own injury either. She had been sacrificing herself for everyone else for far too long. She needed them as much as they needed her.

He closed the door, and started heading up the walkway when he heard Ike say hello. He waved to him and then headed inside.

Michaela was probably working in the kitchen. After finishing the living room, hallway, and attic, her next job was the kitchen.

He could hear the hammering, and also the soft music coming from that direction.

He called out to her.

"Michaela, it's Jake."

"Come on in," she called to him as she came into sight.

It was too difficult to hide his laugh at the sight of her. She was drenched. A quick glance to where the sink remained and he saw the culprit.

"What happened?"

"Go ahead, laugh. I know you want to." She wrung out her T-shirt. He could see her hot pink bra through the wet light pink top. As she carried on about the plumbing in the rotted washer between the pipes and the amount of water that sprayed the place, he just stared at her in awe. She was so damn sexy when she was fired up.

"You should just take off the top. It's see-through now anyway," he teased.

She scrunched her eyebrows at him and began to exit the room, but he grabbed her wrist, lifted her up by her hips, and placed her on the one remaining counter.

Taking position between her legs, he cupped her cheeks and hair and stared at her.

"Calm down, I was just teasing you. You look sexy, baby. Absolutely sexy. Even with your temper flared."

She pulled her bottom lip between her teeth. "I'm mad, Jake."

He smiled. "Obviously." He pressed closer and then leaned down and kissed her deeply. When he felt the cold water against his dry uniform shirt he released her lips.

"I brought over some lunch, but if you need help changing your clothes, I could have you as an appetizer." He nipped at her earlobe, and she swatted his arm.

"Jake, you're on duty."

"I'm on lunch. I could eat you right up." He licked along her neck and nibbled her skin, loving the taste of her sweet skin.

"I'm going to get you all wet. How are you going to explain that at work?" she asked, running her palms up and down his chest.

"I'm the sheriff. I don't need to explain shit. Besides, everyone knows where I am. Remember, my brothers and I are making it known that you're ours."

She widened her eyes and he kissed her again. This time she wrapped her arms around his neck and kissed him back.

When he slowly released her lips, she looked so relaxed and calm.

"I need to change."

He pulled her up into his arms and squeezed her ass. "I'll help you."

He started carrying her toward the stairs when she started laughing. "You don't have time for that. What's in the bag you brought over?"

"I definitely have time for that, and lunch is in the bag. But you only get it if you're a good girl and let me have a little taste of you."

She gave his arm a smack again, just as they entered her bedroom. Slowly he lowered her feet to the rug and then reached for the hem of her shirt.

She grabbed his hands. "Jake?"

"Easy now, sugar. Just a little taste, and then we'll go downstairs and have some lunch. Arms up," he told her, and she pulled that lip of hers between her teeth as she slowly raised her arms up. Sure enough, the prettiest dark pink bra he'd ever seen encased her breasts. The tightness of the bra caused a deep cleavage and he reached up and trailed a finger down the center of the mounds.

"This is a really pretty color on you."

"You think so?" she asked, staring up at him, holding his gaze.

"Better than a plain old white one, I think." He pressed his fingers into the cup and maneuvered her breast from confinement.

Michaela gasped.

"You're so damn sexy."

"I like different color bras, and even panties."

"Panties, too? That's a shame." He used his other hand to undo her shorts and press them down her thighs.

"Why?" She asked him.

"Because you won't be needing panties around my brothers and me."

He gently released her breast and pressed her toward the bed. She fell back and landed on her forearms and elbows as he knelt onto the floor in front of her.

"Let me pleasure you," he said, caressing his palms up her thighs as he reached for the matching pink panties. He pulled them down and Michaela moaned. Her thighs were shaking, and she looked so scared, yet aroused.

He wrapped his hand gently around one ankle as he held her gaze. It turned him on to be able to wrap his large hand around her ankle just so. One look at Michaela, and it seemed to be having the same effect on her.

"Open for me. Offer me your pretty, wet pussy," he told her as he held her gaze and tapped his thumb against her pussy lips.

"Oh, Jake, you're too much. You're wild."

He shook his head. "You do it to me. I want you so badly. Let me have this at least." He pressed his thumb firmer against her clit and she moaned.

"Yes," she whispered and parted her thighs.

Jake maneuvered a finger between her pussy lips and then thrust one finger up into her pussy. "Raise your feet up to the edge of the bed."

She did. He pulled his one finger out and added another digit. In and out he stroked her pussy and watched his fingers glisten with her cum.

"Oh, Jake." She moaned and began to move her hips against his fingers.

He leaned forward and licked her pussy lips.

"Jake!" she squealed, and then tilted up while she pressed her hips back and forth against his tongue. Her pussy leaked more cream, and he suckled every ounce, unwilling to let any escape, and wanting more of her delicious honey.

She was moving on the bed. Her thighs were spread, her ass over the edge. Using his other finger, he wiped some of her cream to her anus, and she gasped.

"What are you doing?"

"Exploring, baby. You know that when we all make love together, we're going to be in every hole." He flicked his tongue against her pussy again, licking, stroking her clit, and then sucking on it.

"Oh damn, that feels incredible," she admitted, and he smiled but continued to bring her pleasure.

"We'll take turns fucking this sweet, tight, virgin pussy, that pretty, sexy mouth of yours, and of course this round, sexy ass." He pressed a finger against her anus and pushed through. In and out he stroked both her pussy and her ass as Michaela exploded.

"Jake, my God, what are you doing to me? I've never felt anything like this before. I feel so wild and naughty."

He chuckled against her belly. "You are being naughty, and the naughtier you are, the more spankings this tight ass will get."

He thrust faster into her ass and pussy as Michaela tossed her head side to side and then screamed out another release.

Easing his fingers from her ass and cunt, he leaned forward and licked her pussy, plunging his tongue inside for more.

"Oh, Jake, I can't take it. It's too much."

She reached for his head, and he gripped her wrist and held them at her sides as he tasted, suckled, licked, and feasted on her pussy until she was wiggling and screaming another release.

He was overwhelmed with emotion. He cared so much for Michaela already, and every little bit of trust she gave him heightened that arousal and need for her to be theirs.

He pulled her to him and hugged her. She immediately hugged him back as they both panted.

"Thank you for trusting me, Michaela."

She cupped his cheeks, and he stared into her eyes and saw her excitement.

"Thank you, for being patient with me."

He reached up from his hold on her thigh and hip, caressed up her ribs to her breast, and stared at her beautiful breasts.

"I can't wait to make love to you, and I know my brothers can't either."

"I know, Jake. I'm just trying to find the confidence needed to take the chance. It's hard to explain."

He knew she was struggling. He reached up and gently rubbed his thumb along the scarring from the gunshot wound.

Then he looked up at her and he saw the tears in her eyes.

"Take as long as you need. We're not going anywhere. We only want you, and you can trust us to be here for you always." He leaned forward and pressed a soft kiss over her scar, and then Michaela hugged him tight, stealing his heart and his breath away.

* * * *

As Jake was leaving the house, Hal arrived carrying a box. He said hello to Jake and then smiled at Michaela. She was blushing and he wondered what the two of them had been up to before he arrived.

He squinted at her. "Come over here."

She pulled her bottom lip between her teeth and slowly approached.

He set the box down on the rug and then pulled her into his arms and kissed her. She squeezed him tight and then kept her cheek against his chest. He smiled at Jake.

"Back to work?"

"Yep, just stopped by for some appetizers and lunch." He tipped his hat as he winked.

Michaela gave his arm a smack.

"Sorry, baby, but you are too tasty not to share with my brothers. I'll see you later."

Jake left the house, closing the door behind him, and Hal looked down at Michaela.

"I take it some progress has been made in the trust department?"

She reached up and placed her hand against his cheek. "Maybe a little." Hal turned his face into her hand and kissed the palm. "What's in the box?"

"A surprise."

She stepped from his arms and placed her hand on the railing of the stairs. He watched as she glided her hand along the spindles and of course the empty spot at the end where a fancy wooden finial was missing. The one on the other side was broken. She had been upset about that.

"The stairs look incredible. I can't believe how quickly you fixed them. Are you going to restain them soon?"

"I don't know. I'm not sure yet."

"Well, maybe some inspiration is needed to finish them off."

"Inspiration?" she asked.

"Check that box."

She sat down on the bottom of the step and he walked closer, leaning on the spot where the finial was missing. Michaela opened up the box and began undoing the tissue paper. It was old and the last layers wrapped in old newspaper. As she uncovered the very fancy wooden finials, Michaela gasped, covered her mouth, and stared up at him.

"Hal, how did you? Where did you find this?"

He knelt down and took the finial from her hand. "Let's just say, I know people."

She looked so excited and happy his heart soared. It was obvious that his gift touched her heart, and she stood up and jumped into his arms, straddling his waist. He stood up straighter, and held her tight as she hugged him.

"You guys just keep amazing me. You'll make it so that I can never leave Treasure Town."

He cupped her cheek and she stared up into his eyes.

"We'll never let you go as is. Now kiss me, and tell me how perfect I am," he teased.

"You are perfect, Hollywood. Now how about you help me install these finials and then pick out a stain to use?

"Putting me to work again?"

"Of course. Are you complaining?"

"Well, I could use a little incentive."

She stared up into his eyes and then licked her lower lip.

"How about a little make-out session and then we get to work?"

He was surprised by her response but he quickly smiled, squeezing her to him. "Sure thing, and how about some of the appetizers you shared with Jake?" He stroked his fingers between the V of her thighs. Michaela turned a nice shade of red.

But before she could change her mind, he tossed her onto his shoulder and ran with her up the stairs, all while she reprimanded him and then finally started laughing.

* * * *

"Michaela, do you have a minute? I'd love for you to meet my family," Chief Martelli said as she delivered some drinks to a nearby table.

"Sure thing, Chief. How are you?"

"I'm doing well. How is the house coming along?"

"Well, I guess considering that you haven't had to respond to any more fires at it, I'm making progress."

He chuckled. "Thank goodness for that. This is my wife, Angelina, my daughter, Serefina, and my sons."

"Oh, we met before. Eddie, Lance, and Tyler, right?" she asked as she pointed to each one and then shook their hands. They all smiled. "Serefina, thank you so much for sending over the bagels and pastries last week. That was very kind of you and the owners of Sullivan's."

Serefina stood up next to Michaela and smiled. "Not a problem. I was happy to hear that the fire was minor and things seem to be going more smoothly now."

"Well, I only had a minor run-in with a plumbing issue," she said and then chuckled.

"Oh, that doesn't sound good," Eddie stated.

"Well, I'm not made out of paper so I survived it."

"Damn, that sounds crazy. One of my boyfriends, Ice, has a friend who is a great plumber," Serefina stated, and Michaela smiled. The comment about boyfriends in the plural came so naturally out of her mouth, and no one batted an eye at that. Not even her parents, never mind her brothers. The more time she spent around the people in Treasure Town, the more she liked it. Ménage relationships were definitely accepted around here.

"Hey, beautiful, can you come on over to that table right there and take our drink order?" some guy asked as he placed his hand on her hip. She pushed it down and off of her and smiled.

"Sure, just give me a moment please."

"For you, anything." He winked and then headed back over to the table with about five guys. They were laughing and having a good time, and they were watching their friend who just approached her.

"Watch yourself over there, Michaela. Those guys have been drinking a bunch," Eddie stated. He and his brothers as well as the Chief were giving the guy who came over dirty looks when he approached Michaela.

"I'll be fine. I'm really supposed to be behind the bar anyway. Well, back to work. It was nice meeting you, Angelina and Serefina."

"Hey, we should hang out sometime. I can show you all the great shopping places in the area. There's a cute boutique across town," Serefina said.

"Oh, that would be nice. I'll let you know." Serefina waved, but then some big guy came up behind her, wrapped his arm around her waist, and kissed her cheek. Serefina smiled wide and turned into the man's arms.

"That's Ace, one of her boyfriends. There's Bull and Ice over there talking to the sheriff," the chief told her. She looked at the two men but only briefly as her eyes landed on the sheriff. He was talking to his dad. She would be sure to go over and say hello.

She said good-bye and then headed to the table of guys.

They started giving their orders, throwing in flirtatious comments, and she laughed at them but remained professional.

"Anything else?" she asked, and one of the guys, a tall one, reached for her hair and caressed the ponytail.

"Is that a belly ring I see?" he asked her.

"Want to release my hair?"

"Maybe. Or maybe I'd like to see that move you did on the loser who held you hostage in the sheriff's department."

She was shocked that he brought it up, but then she swallowed her anger and tried to calm the potential situation.

She gave her head a turn, making the ponytail slide from his fingers. Placing her hands on her hips, she stared up into his eyes.

"Honey, I'm going to forget that you said that, and I'm going to fill this drink order, and send over the waitress who is working your section. You're going to be cool, and you're going to be respectful, and everyone is going to have a good time tonight."

The "oohs" and "ahhs" went through the small crowd, drawing attention to them and her.

He placed his hand on her hip again. "I especially like the way you straddled his hips, and how your skirt was up to your waist revealing these long sexy thighs of yours." He caressed his hand down her thigh, and she swatted it away.

When he went to reach for her wrist to grab it, she counter moved, twisted him around and then took his legs out from underneath him. He fell onto the floor on his ass. Before he could get up, Bear was there, as the guy's friends roared with laughter.

"Stay down, asshole. It's all over," Bear yelled at the guy.

Michaela smiled at the other guys. "I'll go get your drinks. Behave now."

"Yes, ma'am," one of them replied, wide eyed, and everyone seemed to go about their business.

Michaela was filling the order and getting it ready for the other waitress working the floor to handle and deliver. But it was crowded and appeared that she would have to face that jerk again. Maybe he wouldn't be so stupid.

"Are you okay?" Burt asked her. She looked at him and raised her eyebrows.

He chuckled. "Okay, I get it. That was real sweet that move you did."

"Thanks. I'm going to go deliver these drinks and then I'll be back behind the bar."

"I could have someone else deliver them."

They looked around.

"It's too busy. Don't worry, I got it." She carried the tray of drinks from behind the bar and walked over to the table. She started handing out the drinks, and the one guy who messed with her was staring at her.

"Sorry I was a jerk."

"That's okay, we're all allowed to be jerks every once in a while." She smiled and then he smiled.

"Is it true that you're seeing the McCurrans?"

She squinted her eyes and then felt the arm move around her midsection. The guy's eyes widened, and then someone said, "Hello, Bear."

She released a sigh of relief and tilted her head to see him standing way above her.

"Everything okay over here?"

"Of course," she replied.

"Okay, have a good time."

They watched her as Bear took her hand and led her back to the bar.

As she stood next to the entrance to the bar, she turned and crossed her arms in front of her chest. He eyed over her cleavage and knew the top was low, but that was part of getting good tips.

"Are you happy now? Is word out that I belong to the McCurran men?" she asked, and he gave a sly smiled.

He looked around them. She did, too, and could see some people watching them.

"I think so, but I better make it clear, especially with you wearing this top."

"What's wrong with this—"

He pulled her close and kissed her deeply, cutting off her words and making it clear that she definitely belonged to the McCurran men.

* * * *

Bear followed Michaela out of the parking lot of the bar. She had given him a wave the moment she exited the building and grabbed her bike. She spotted him immediately and that calmed his concern. He wasn't stalking her. He was just worried about some guy trying something.

After the incident in The Station tonight and the mention of the video, he kept thinking that some guy or guys might try to hurt her or challenge her. He couldn't leave. Not until he knew she was safely home. She seemed to be able to handle herself, and that was reassuring. But why should she have to? A woman as beautiful and sweet as Michaela shouldn't always be defending herself against some guy with a gun, or a drunk in a bar challenging her, and preying on her femininity. That shit really pissed him off.

Bear followed in his truck and watched her pedaling the bike. Those damn short shorts she wore accentuated her ass and her thighs. Every up and down motion she made as she pedaled while standing up gave him a harder cock.

He imagined what it would be like when she rode him as they made love. He could play with her plump, sexy breasts as he glided in and out of her.

He gripped the steering wheel tighter as she approached the street to her house. He felt obsessed. His feelings for her were growing every day. He missed her and thought about her at work. To see her tonight, to know how late she would be getting home and that the chances of seeing her were slim, bothered him. He wanted to hold her in his arms, get to know everything about her, and see where this attraction led.

He parked the truck and got out. She was getting off the bike. His eyes roamed over her ass, and she turned to look at him.

She crinkled her eyebrows as she placed the bike onto the front porch.

"Billy, are you okay?"

He looked her over and felt the need to hold her become overwhelming. Her shirt was slightly lifted, revealing a belly ring and her flat belly. She wasn't too thin, and had toned arms and great, muscular legs. Probably from all the physical work she did.

He walked up the steps and met her by the front door.

"Billy?" she whispered.

He pulled her into his arms, lifted her up, and pressed her against the front door.

"Baby, did I tell you how much I missed you today?"

She began to shake her head, obviously shocked by his move, and he leaned down to kiss her.

As that kiss instantly grew deeper, he couldn't seem to get close enough to her. He plastered his hand over her ass, squeezing, massaging, and letting his fingers stroke her pussy from behind. She lifted her hips and allowed him to touch her over the material of the damn jean shorts.

His cock felt about ready to burst through the damn zipper of his jeans, he was so aroused. And then she ran those damn delicate fingers of hers through his shoulder-length hair, and he lost it.

Pulling his mouth from hers and kissing along her neck, he squeezed her tighter. "You drive me wild. Let's go inside." He continued to kiss and lick her skin.

She grabbed onto his hair and stared into his eyes. "Billy, we need to slow down."

He was disappointed. Hell, he was never in this type of position before. Michaela wasn't like other women he'd known. She was fearful, resistant to trust, and he needed to put on the breaks and work at gaining that trust, not bulldozing over it.

He slowly pressed his forehead to hers.

"Well then, I guess we should say good night."

She swallowed hard and looked disappointed. That was a good thing.

"Because if I come in your house, I can't promise to keep my hands off of you."

She smiled. "Don't think for one second that I don't feel the same way about you. You're such a good-looking man, Billy. You're so big and strong and sweet."

"Sweet?" he asked, cringing from the wimpy term.

She chuckled and then tugged his hair in a playful manner. "Sweet is good, Billy. Sweet and compassionate and caring. Those are all great qualities that you and your brothers share. But it is late, and you worked all day, I worked all night, and we both have work again tomorrow. I appreciate that you stayed and followed me home. But I can take care of myself, you know?"

He cupped her ass and pressed her snugly against the door. "Oh, I know all right. I was there tonight, at The Station, when you knocked that guy on his ass."

"And I appreciate that you came over before he decided to do something stupid."

"Laying his hands on you was stupid. I was worried, and well, jealous."

"Jealous? Why, Billy? I wasn't flirting. You know I don't date. Heck, you and your brothers have been very patient and taking your time getting to know me. It's helping and I don't want some stupid drunk guy to ruin what we have."

"We have something?" he asked and gave a small smile. Michaela smiled wide, and then ran her hands over his shoulders and snuggled closer. Her lips were inches from his.

"Oh, we have something. A beginning. Now kiss me good night, and get home to bed so you're in top condition for work tomorrow."

"Yes, ma'am." He kissed her softly, imagining and hoping that one day he and his brothers would share her bed, and come home to Michaela.

* * * *

"So what do you think? Are we making progress?" Billy asked Hal as they finished getting dressed after taking showers, after work. It was Thursday night, and every night for the past couple of weeks except for Friday and Saturday when Michaela worked at The Station, they would visit her. Jake would stop in and have lunch with her, and then tell them about their conversations.

In those two weeks they had grown fonder of her, but still couldn't seem to get her to divulge information about the gunshot wound, her past, her family if she had any, or her plans of remaining in Treasure Town.

"I think so. I mean tonight she asked that we come over for dinner. The house is still under construction but that hasn't stopped us from seeing her."

"I'm looking forward to it. I miss her during the day. Isn't that crazy?" Billy admitted.

Hal smiled. "I do, too. I think it's because this is the real deal. No bullshit. I'll feel a hundred percent better about the four of us once I know for sure that she's not lying about anything. I know she has the right to keep her own secrets, or to not share everything about herself, but after Lisa, I need that reassurance."

"Me, too. Maybe we'll make some progress tonight."

They headed downstairs and Jake was there.

"You two ready or what?"

"Let's go," Billy said and they headed over to Michaela's.

* * * *

"His name is Clyde Duvall. He's a tracker, Michaela, and he may have been hired by Solomon," Alonso stated over the phone.

"A tracker? You mean to help find me?"

"Yes. He was last seen in Jersey City. Do you remember that little apartment you stayed at until you discovered Treasure Town? Well, he located it, questioned the landlord at the place you stayed."

"Oh God. Does this mean I should leave? Relocate?"

"I don't think so. The Feds are close to finding Dipero. He's the shooter. He was sighted in New York City. There's a good chance that they'll catch him."

"So what do you think Solomon and this tracker want?"

"Either to find you before Dipero does, or to help finish the job the killer didn't accomplish. But I can't see why he would help Dipero when Dipero was sent to collect money owed and to kill Solomon. There's more to this situation. The Feds think so, too. I can't get into all the leads we're working on, but I'm hoping something pans out quickly. I may not have a choice, Michaela. I may need to contact that sheriff friend of yours sooner than later."

"Oh God, I don't want them to know. I was just beginning to feel safe with them and here in this town." Alonso was the closest thing she had that could be considered a friend and someone she sort of trusted. Well, she did trust him because she'd just informed him about Jake, Billy, and Hal and the ménage thing. He wasn't as shocked as she thought he would be. Then he told her about his sister, Maria, and her three husbands. They lived out in Texas.

"I still think that you need to be careful. Have you told them anything about New York, and about Carlucci and Solomon?"

"Of course I haven't told them. It's not an easy conversation to have. I'm still not sure if I should get involved with them. Besides, I might have to leave in a hurry, so it may be better to remain friends and nothing more. Especially with the information you just shared with me. I'm scared."

"Michaela, if what you've told me about them is all true, what they've done, the empathy, the compassion, I'd say you were crazy not to take a chance. Hell, you deserve happiness."

"I appreciate that, Alonso, but how can I take that risk when there's still a bull's-eye on my forehead? When there's another man, a tracker, trying to find me?"

She heard the floor creak and looked back toward the kitchen door of the house and saw Jake standing there. Billy and Hal were right behind him.

She swallowed hard as she closed up the grill she was cooking on.

"I need to go. Please keep me posted, and I'll call you if I think it's time to move. Bye."

Michaela put down the phone.

"Hi, I didn't even hear you come in." She turned back toward the grill. The chicken she'd made was all finished. She just needed to baste it one more time with BBQ sauce.

She was doing that as the guys walked onto the deck.

She felt the hand on her shoulder, move under her hair, and she turned up toward Jake as he cupped her face between his hands.

He just stared down into her eyes as she placed her hands over his wrists.

"What's wrong?"

Billy took the brush and continued to baste the chickens. "I'll do this."

"They're done. I can take them off."

"Let Billy," Jake said and then pulled her into an embrace.

She hugged him back and knew that they heard her conversation. Perhaps subconsciously she called Alonso and had this conversation and hoped that the guys arrived. Maybe if they heard more about it this way than through her having to explain, it would be easier. But somehow it wasn't easier. It was harder.

Billy removed the chickens and then closed up the grill. Hal covered the chicken with foil as they turned off the gas.

Jake walked her over toward the set of wicker furniture that Jake helped her pick up and deliver to the house yesterday. It was slightly damaged and people were giving it away, but she fixed it up, spray-painted it brown to look like real rattan, and then made some cushions for them as well.

They sat down on the love seat, and Billy and Hal joined them.

"Okay, it's been two weeks since we talked about patience, commitment, and trust. I admit that my patience is growing slim, but now there's no more left. Not when I hear you talking on the phone and saying that you may be leaving, especially with a bull's-eye on your forehead."

She started to speak, but he gave her one of his stern expressions, and with Billy and Hal as backup, she knew to choose her battles wisely. They were intimidating.

"No more stalling. No more secrets, just God's honest truth, Michaela. It's all we're asking for. The truth."

She took a deep breath and looked at the three of them. "Okay. The truth." She stood up and Jake turned as if prepared to grab her to stop her if he needed to. But he wouldn't have to. She wanted to tell them. She wanted them to hear the truth.

"You heard right. The whole bull's-eye thing is true. Someone may be looking for me."

Billy and Hal began to ask questions but Jake cut them off. His firm voice and authoritative personality came through and took over.

"Who?" he asked.

"The same man who shot me in the chest."

* * * *

Jake stood up and ran his fingers through his hair while his brothers sat there in shock.

"Who's the guy? What's his name? Who is Alonso?" Jake asked.

She shook her head as she clasped her hands on her lap.

He stepped toward her with his hands on his waist, trying to remain calm when all he wanted to do was demand that she tell him every single detail so he could protect her.

"I don't want you involved. I already told the detective. If this guy or guys come looking for me and start getting closer, then I'm gone."

"Bullshit! This is the same guy that fucking shot you in the chest? Who the hell is he? An ex-boyfriend, someone you did business with? Who?" Billy demanded.

"Calm down, Billy," Jake stated.

Michaela leaned back against the porch railing.

"It's not like that. It's a long story."

"We have all night. You're not getting off with saying you don't want us involved. I'm the goddamn sheriff of this town. If there's trouble headed this way, I have the right to know. If someone wants to hurt my woman, our woman, then we have the right to know so that we can protect you."

She shook her head and turned toward him. "No, Jake. Let the detectives and the Feds handle it. I won't let anyone get hurt because of me. It's fine like this. I can leave and move somewhere else. I don't have any family left. I'm used to going solo."

He grabbed her by her arms and held her firmly. "Your days of going solo are over, Michaela. Don't you realize that you're already a part of us, a part of Treasure Town? I can protect you and so can the other men around here."

She shook her head and he could feel her body shaking, too.

"I survived the first time. I won't survive the second. He'll make certain."

"Michaela, you've never lived in this type of town, not one like Treasure Town. These men, these people who live around here, are resilient and they're special. A lot of retired military and some still active. I want you to sit down, and tell us everything. And when I say everything. I mean the entire story, and you're not to leave any detail out. This is not a negotiation. You're going to do it, simply because we care about you, we want you in our lives, and you survived that gunshot wound so that we could meet and be together. Now sit down, get comfortable, and get at it," Billy said.

Jake had to hide his chuckle. This was so not Billy. He was never confrontational or demanding. It was part of the reason he was called Bear besides his obvious size. He was calm and gentle, but if you messed with him, he was a force to reckon with.

Michaela must have taken him seriously, because she walked over to the couch and sat down.

* * * *

Billy was shocked, and Michaela didn't leave anything out. From her tough childhood, her issues with abandonment, and her need to try and hold on to the only family she had, her sister, she was a fighter. That was obvious by her multiple attempts at trying to secure a relationship with her sister, her last living relative. It was also apparent in her surviving a bullet wound to her chest initiated by a man who was hired by someone to kill her sister's boyfriend.

"So why are they still after you? You survived, there was evidence left at the scene, the cops know this guy did it, and your sister's boyfriend was part of it. Why go after you?"

"I guess because the guy who hired the hit man will be afraid that the hit man might turn on him to save his ass. I don't know. Don Dipero is ruthless. He's wanted by the Feds anyway, and it seems to Alonso that he could be involved with some other things. Political stuff. Who knows? And Solomon owed Carlucci money, so maybe if Solomon found me first and brought me to the hit man then his debt may be lessened? I really don't know, but I'm not planning on meeting any of them to find out."

"Wait, you said Dipero?"

She nodded her head.

"Shit, the mug shot and picture were sent to the department."

She stood up.

"Oh God, they think he's come this far?"

"No, I don't know, baby, it's standard protocol when someone is on the run from authority. Especially if the Feds are involved, too. I read the case file. This guy is bad news."

"How did you survive getting shot?" Hal asked.

She told them about surprise visiting her sister, Annette, and how they were talking when the hit man arrived.

"She didn't want me there. She was basically telling me to leave her alone and to never contact her again."

"Do you think she may have been trying to protect you? Maybe she knew that her boyfriend was in trouble?" Jake asked.

She shook her head and swallowed hard, as if her emotions were getting in the way of speaking.

"She didn't care. She didn't want me there when Solomon arrived. She thought that I would tell him about her past, her dealings with drugs and prostitution."

"Prostitution?" Billy asked.

"She was a screwed-up kid. Like I explained, our childhoods weren't good. She took off and I was left handling the leftover crap. I really don't need to rehash that, Billy. It's done and over with. It's in the past. When I refused to leave and made one last attempt at trying to save our relationship, Annette told me she wanted nothing to do with me and that Solomon was all she cared about. She told me that I didn't exist in her eyes and that I needed to leave and never contact her again.

"The hit man showed up, and she didn't even try to protect me or put herself in front of me. She defended Solomon and refused to say where he was. He pointed the gun at her and shot her twice, right in front of me. I should have died there, too, but the door opened, Solomon was there, saw the guy with the gun, and took off. The gunman pointed and shot as he ran from the room, but I turned left to duck down instead of right, so the bullet hit me in the right chest bone instead of the left and through my heart. Somehow I survived surgery. This guy, this hit man, would have killed anyone in his path to get to Solomon."

"Jesus. What else do you have on this guy, Jake?" Hal asked.

"He's got a long rap sheet, from what information I got through the department. He's a ruthless killer and is wanted in questioning in numerous murder cases. "

"He's relentless. He ransacked my place out in Chicago. After I got out of the hospital, Alonso had the local department check it out first. That's what got me to remain in New York and train before moving on my own. This tracker guy, Duvall, apparently just found the place I stayed for a week in Jersey City."

"Shit. What does Alonso think? Does he want to move you again?"

She shook her head. "He said they were working with the Feds on some leads that he hoped panned out. I'm not sure though. I mean, I moved back into the city for a month to train, so if he is tracking me, that would be the next place he would go. Eventually he'll come here."

"Train?" Hal asked.

"The self-defense stuff? Who taught you?" Jake asked.

"Alonso. We became good friends. Without him I wouldn't have survived the psychological trauma, never mind the physical. He's been keeping me abreast of any sightings and is in close contact with the Feds working the case."

Billy caressed her cheek. "Just a friend, or was there more between you two?"

She held his gaze. "Just friends, Billy. You heard about my life. Do you really think I could handle a boyfriend or getting intimate with anyone with such trust issues?"

He squinted his eyes at her. "What are you saying?" he asked.

She shyly looked down and then back up. "What do you think I'm saying?"

Billy's eyes widened and then he leaned over and kissed her softly on the lips.

As he parted his lips from hers he smiled. "We're going to take good care of you. You're going to be our woman, and the convincing starts right now."

* * * *

Billy took Michaela's hand and pulled her onto his lap. Wearing the pretty skirt and blouse, he lifted her so she would straddle his waist. As he drew her in for a kiss, he ran his palms up her thighs and under the skirt. He moved them back down and then caressed along her waist to her neck. He held her neck and head beneath her hair and kissed her deeply, allowing his emotions and desires to show. He held nothing back, and neither did Michaela.

She kissed him back and their make-out session began. He maneuvered his palms along her thighs, under the skirt to her panties. From the feel of them, they were thin, barely there and instantly his cock was hard and aroused. She must have been, too, as she lifted up, giving him better access to her body. Cupping her ass cheek in one hand while maneuvering the other to draw her even snugger against him, he heard her moan. She rocked her hips on his lap until he released his hold on her and began to unbutton the buttons on the blouse.

She didn't stop him, but instead began to undo the buttons on his shirt, and then caress her palms over his bare chest while she hungrily kissed him.

In a flash he was pulling off her blouse and then her camisole below. Behind her, Jake undid the clasp of her bra and she eased her arms out before grabbing back onto Billy to continue to kiss him. But Billy had another plan, as he caressed his palms from her waist to her ribs and breasts, absorbing the feel of her half-naked in his arms.

He eased his mouth off her lips and trailed his tongue and teeth along her collarbone and neck. As he cupped one luscious breast, he made his way toward the other with lips and tongue. She moaned and tiled her head back as he attempted to suckle as much of her breast as he could into his mouth.

"Oh, Billy. That feels so good." She thrust her hips up and down on his lap.

He released her breast with a plop. "I don't want to stop. I want all of you."

She held his gaze, and then Jake reached under her hair, gripped it, and turned her head up toward him. Her lips parted as she knelt upward so she could reach him better.

"We want you, together." Before she could answer, Jake kissed her deeply, so Billy used the opportunity to reach under her skirt. He maneuvered between her legs under her panties and pushed them aside. Before he could thrust a finger into her cunt, Michaela was lowering onto his digit, trying to ride it.

"Holy shit, baby, you're so sexy," Billy said as he thrust his fingers up into her.

Jake was devouring her moans, and now Hal joined in. He moved in behind Michaela and lifted her skirt. Billy assumed that he began playing with her ass, because suddenly she shot forward, pulled from Jake's mouth, and cried out an orgasm.

"Oh, Hal. Oh my God, what are you doing to me?"

"Getting this ass ready for cock. That's what you want, don't you, baby? Me, Billy, and Jake, inside you at the same time?"

"Oh God, I don't think I can. I don't know." She started panting between breaths. She was so aroused, and her nipples were incredibly hard.

"We need more room. Let's get her to the bedroom," Jake said. Billy stood up, still holding her in his arms as if she weighed nothing at all.

* * * *

She wanted to make love to them. She trusted them, she felt safe with them, and hell, she was in love with them already, so what did anything else matter? But her nerves were beginning to challenge her free spirit as Billy, Jake, and Hal removed their clothing.

She stared at Hal, as he undressed the quickest. His blue eyes sparkled as he curled one finger toward her asking her to come closer. She eased slowly toward his naked body, her eyes widening at the sight of his thick, hard cock.

She gulped as he stepped right in front of her and eased the rest of her skirt off of her.

Her mouth was inches from his pectoral muscles. The dips and ridges combined with the intricate tattoos along his chest and shoulder were aphrodisiacs.

"Touch him. We're yours to explore," Billy told her as he stood behind her and pushed her hair to the side. He laid his lips against her neck, and she felt Billy's cock tap against her ass cheeks.

She shivered with desire and anticipation.

Hal ran his palm along her waist to her breast. He cupped it, massaged it tenderly, and then leaned down and licked the tip.

She reached for his arm, tilted her head back, and moaned.

It was amazing how hungry and wild she became.

"Baby, are you on birth control?" Jake asked. And thank God he did, because she wasn't even thinking straight.

She chuckled. "Yes, I am."

Hal reached fingers downward and stroked her cunt, making her gasp. She didn't want them to think she was experienced. She needed slow, even though her pussy seemed to want it fast.

She cleared her throat, and held Hal's wrist as he thrust two fingers up into her cunt. Billy was stroking her anus and rubbing against her.

She panicked. "I'm on birth control because of the bad periods."

Billy kissed her neck. "It's one of the benefits, right?" he asked, as he continued to kiss her neck and fondle her anus. She was losing her mind. She wasn't bringing up a scientific conversation on birth control. She was trying to tell them that she was a virgin.

"Arms up," Hal told her as Jake reached for her arms and lifted them. He held them up by her wrists, as Billy and Hal lowered to their knees in front of her. They parted her thighs. She stepped outward and her pussy erupted, dripping cream down her pussy as well as her inner thighs. Billy swiped a finger over the cream and pressed it to her anus as Hal thrust fingers into her cunt.

"Oh God!" she moaned.

Jake cupped and massaged her breasts with one hand as he remained holding both of her wrists in the other hand. She felt so overpowered and helpless, yet so damn sexy and desirable.

"You are so ready for cock, aren't you, sweetheart?" Hal asked and then leaned forward and licked where his fingers plunged into.

"Oh, Hal, oh, that feels incredible."

"I got something else for you that's incredible," Hal stated, as he used his free hand to stroke his long, thick cock.

"Get her to the bed. She's ready for us," Hal announced.

In a flash Jake was carrying her over to the bed. Hal was lying down, legs spread over the edge with open arms. His cock glistened with pre-cum and for some strange reason she wished she wasn't on birth control and could bear their children. She wasn't even a person who wanted children or a family, especially after her fucked-up childhood. Until these men. These three, magnificent, sexy men changed her entire outlook on life.

Hal fisted his cock in his hands as Jake set her down over him. She gripped his shoulders as he tried to align his cock with her entrance.

She paused and he scrunched his eyes up at her. She felt Jake behind her stroking his cock against her anus. Billy came up onto the bed, stroking his cock, taking up the entire right side of the bed with his full large muscles, tattoos along his shoulder and arm, and his shoulder-length hair just begging to be pulled.

"I need to tell the three of you something."

Jake kissed her shoulder, Bear ran a fingernail along her breast and nipple, and Hal squeezed her hip bones, his cock pressed against her pussy lips.

"What is it, baby? We need you so badly," Billy told her.

Her cheeks warmed. "I need the three of you so badly, too. You just need to know that I trust each of you. I feel so safe with each of you. I've never done this before and I've never felt safe enough until now."

"Michaela, what do you mean never done this before?" Hal asked.

Jake gripped her shoulders and pulled her slightly back and against his chest, she could feel the ridge f his cock between her ass cheeks.

"You're a virgin?" Jake asked, and she nodded her head as she tilted her head back to hold his gaze. He pressed a palm against her cheeks and smiled. "We're honored to be your firsts, and your only." Then he kissed her, and she felt his large, comforting hand over her waist along with Hal's finger stroking her nipple and Billy's hand caress her thigh. They were all touching her, and that was when she felt most secure and right.

* * * *

Hal maneuvered his hands along her ribs and to her breasts. Their woman was gorgeous, sexy, and so reserved. He couldn't believe for one moment that he or anyone could compare her to Lisa, and what she had done to them. He was relieved that she was on the pill, but of course still wondered if she lied. Lisa made him distrustful in that area. He closed his eyes and blocked the weakening, insecure thoughts from his head. This was Michaela, not Lisa. Michaela was honest, sweet, and originally untrusting due to her own experiences with people she couldn't rely on. She could rely on them, and he most definitely could rely on her.

"Look at me, Michaela," Hal whispered.

She turned from Jake and looked down toward Hal. He smiled and her blue eyes lit up.

"One day real soon, we're going to share a story with you. An experience that hardened our hearts, and cut us off from making that deep, intimate connection with someone, until now." He smiled.

She scrunched her eyes up and leaned forward, causing her pussy, wet and warm, to glide over the tip of his cock. It was right there, partially in, just one push and her virginity would belong to them forever.

"Someone hurt you that you trusted?" she asked.

He reached up and cupped her cheek as Jake ran his hand along her back and shoulder and Billy caressed her hair. She looked at Billy and then over her shoulder at Jake with an expression of care and concern.

"It doesn't matter now. All that matters is you and us. We're ready, are you?" Hal asked.

She licked her lips, letting her tongue peek out and glide along them. He slowly lifted upward and she pressed down.

"Yes. Make love to me. All of you, together."

She eased her pussy down his shaft as he pushed upward. Their eyes were locked, hers slightly closing as he felt his cock push through the barrier. She gasped and moved forward and he sank deeper into her.

"So tight, so very good," Hal told her. She hugged his shoulders and rubbed her breasts along his chest, and so it began, as they made love slowly until she adjusted to him.

* * * *

Billy watched in awe as Hal made love to Michaela first. But he and his brothers were so close it was like they were making love to her together already.

He reached over and caressed her hair as Hal thrust upward. When she looked at him with passion and sexiness in her eyes, he smiled wide, while stroking his cock.

"Together. We need you."

She nodded her head and he stood on his knees stroking his cock. She licked her lips as she stared at it, and his dick responded by growing thicker, harder. He'd never felt so aroused just from a woman eying over his manhood. But here he was ready to shoot his load, and Michaela hadn't even laid hand or mouth on it.

"I've never done that either."

His eyes widened. "Baby, just open up and take a taste. I'm yours, and you've got me so hard and aroused, I know I won't last with that sexy mouth of yours on me."

She licked her lips, and she bent forward as Jake began to caress her ass cheeks.

She closed her eyes as Jake stroked a finger between the crack of her ass. But she trudged onward, opening her mouth and accepting his guidance.

He watched in awe as she licked the tip of his cock, making him shake with desire. "Easy, baby. Nice and easy."

She licked along the base, and then reached out and cupped his balls, making him grip her shoulder.

"Oh shit, Michaela, I'm too sensitive there. Too fucking sensitive."

She squeezed again and then started to suck him down, letting as much of his thick, long cock, slide down her throat that she could.

"A fucking natural. Look at her. She's so sexy," Jake stated, and he did something to her ass, making her moan against Billy's cock. Hal began to thrust a little faster, grunting and moaning her name as he increased the speed.

"She's so wet. Holy shit," Jake said, and then Michaela moaned again.

Jake placed a hand on her shoulder and moved back and forth against her. He locked gazes with Billy.

"She's incredible," Billy whispered.

"Her ass is incredible. She's sucking my finger in, and gripping it tight. I won't last long."

"Do it now, Jake. Fuck her ass before I come." Hal grunted and Michaela moved her head up and down, sucking along Billy's cock.

"Yeah, Michaela. Just like that. Just like that. Oh God, she's incredible. I'm almost there," Billy told them.

"I'm coming in, baby. This tight, round ass is too fucking beautiful." He gave it a smack and she jerked and Hal moaned.

"Fuck, she likes it. Her pussy just leaked some more cream. Holy shit, smack that ass some more," Hal ordered.

* * * *

Jake gave her ass a squeeze and then another smack as he eased his finger in and out of her ass. She was so wet and aroused, he pulled his finger from her ass and swiped some more of her cream from her pussy to her anus.

"Here I come," he whispered next to her shoulder and then slowly pressed his cock between the tight rings.

"Fuck." Billy grabbed a hold of her hair and thrust his cock into her mouth. When he pulled slowly from her lips, he crushed his mouth against hers as she moaned and panted.

Billy fell back onto the bed and Hal began to counterthrust upward into her.

"Oh my God. Oh God," she screamed and then thrust backward against Jake's cock. He gave her ass a smack.

"Easy, baby, I don't want to hurt you."

"Faster. Oh God, I can feel something. It's so intense, so right there. Please move, just like that but deeper, deeper." She was ordering them and Jake lost control. Hal shoved upward and was pinching her nipples as Jake grabbed a hold of her hips and stroked into her ass hard and fast. Her ass cheeks shook and her sexy body looked so tanned and gorgeous. She was their woman. Their mate, their everything.

"Fuck." Hal thrust upward and came inside of her. Jake wrapped an arm around her waist and pulled her back against his chest as he cupped one breast and held on to her with a strong arm. She gripped his arm and leaned her head back giving him even deeper access to her ass.

"Jake. Oh God, what is that?"

"Let go. Let it happen, baby, release it and just let go," Hal told her. Jake thrust into her harder, exploding inside of her as she screamed aloud and shook in his arms as she came.

Instantly his brothers were there kissing her face, her shoulder, her breasts, and everywhere they could. Jake squeezed her to him.

"You're our woman, Michaela. All ours, always." He kissed her neck and felt the powerful sense of unity between the four of them, and just a twinge of fear. She needed them, as much as they all needed her.

Chapter 6

Michaela awoke with her face against Billy's chest and a hand over her ass from behind her. She looked up and saw him staring at the portrait on her wall. She peeked her tongue out and licked his skin, then began kissing along his pectoral muscles as she used her fingers to trace the tattoos on his shoulder and arm. The fingers on her ass squeezed tighter and then maneuvered under her belly to her cunt. She lifted her ass and then felt Jake's lips against her shoulder.

She looked up toward Billy as she lifted her pelvis letting her ass raise higher.

"Where's Hal?" she asked and then gasped as Jake stroked a finger up into her cunt. Jake began to kiss along her ass cheeks and spine, as he pulled her onto her side.

"He's fixing dinner. You must be starving," Billy said as he turned toward her to place his palm against her cheek before he kissed her lips.

"Hmmm, not for food," she said once he released her lips.

Jake maneuvered his head under her thigh and was between her thighs exploring her pussy.

"Jake?" she questioned, and he rolled her fully to her back. He was between her thighs, and Billy was leaning on one shoulder and forearm tracing her nipple with his fingernail.

"I'm hungry for this." Jake stroked her pussy with two fingers eliciting more cream to lubricate his entry.

"Yes," she told him, holding his gaze. He aligned his cock with her pussy and thrust right into her with no preamble. She reached for his wide, strong shoulders and held on as he immediately began to set a fast, hard pace.

He used his thick, hard body to maneuver her to his liking, spreading her thighs wider and higher against his ribs. She absorbed every ounce of the masterpiece making love to her. He was gorgeous, sexy, and big. Muscles, tattoos, and ridges of veins and more muscles dominated his body. His chest was heavy and hard as he pressed against her, deepening every stroke. She ran her hands through his crew cut hair and focused on his blue eyes when she felt her body convulse beneath him. She felt like a broken faucet. With every stroke she fell deeper, madder in love with Jake and with Hal and Billy. It was amazing, but even as she made love with Jake, she felt as if she were making love to Billy and Hal, too.

Jake tightened up and then came inside of her as she moaned her release along with him. She hugged his neck, and he kissed her check, squeezing her body to him, nearly crushing her.

They locked gazes and both smiled.

"You're perfect." He kissed her nose and then she turned toward Billy.

Jake eased off of her and she went to roll toward Billy, prepared to straddle him, but he had a different plan.

* * * *

Billy tuned Michaela around and bent her over on all fours. She was facing the portrait she had painted on the wall. He had stared at it for so long waiting for Michaela to awaken so he could ask her about it.

But right now he had one thing in mind. To make love to Michaela, and brand her his woman.

He ran us hands along her waist as he pressed against her back.

Moving her hair from her neck and face, he whispered and kissed her. "I love this painting. Are you almost finished with it?" he asked her, but all she could do was moan.

"Is it someplace you've been?" He maneuvered his arm around her waist and under her belly to press a finger to her pussy. She was sopping wet and his cock grew even thicker and harder.

"It's Tuscany." She thrust her ass back against his front. He used his other hand to cup her breast and pinch the nipple.

"I like it. The sun is gorgeous and so real looking. It's got beautiful colors, and looks like a photograph."

He pulled his fingers from her pussy, and she gasped until he replaced them with his cock. Easing his way into her cunt from behind, she whispered, "Not real, never been there."

"Well, this is real. This moment, this connection." He grunted as he stroked all the way into her, balls deep. Michaela gripped the comforter and pushed her ass back against him.

"You like how this feels?"

"Yes."

"You want it slow or fast?"

"Fast, hard," she replied, and he smiled.

He reached up and gripped her hair, giving it a slight yank. "Hard and fast, huh?"

"Yes." She moaned, head tilted back, shoulders arched.

"You got it." He slowly pulled out and then thrust back into her. He released his hold and grabbed onto her hips and began a sequence of strokes that made Michaela moan and call his name. The bed was creaking, the depth of his emotions was overwhelming, and she just kept encouraging him.

"Harder, faster, oh God. More, Billy, more."

He thrust faster and harder, gripping her hips and her breasts before he heard her scream her release and her inner muscles tightened like a vise grip on his cock. He roared as he shot his seed into her core, shaking with overexertion.

"Amazing." He kissed her shoulder and caressed her ass. She remained on all fours and he slowly pulled back but absorbed the sight of her body, as he detached his cock from her pussy. She was his, theirs, always. He massaged her ass cheeks and then gave her booty a spank.

"Hey," she reprimanded.

"Hey yourself. You have a great ass, Michaela. One I can't wait to fuck in just a little while."

Her cheeks blushed, and she slid to her belly and curled up with a pillow.

He reached over and caressed along her hip, taking position next to her, lying on the bed.

He gently massaged her arm and then her thigh, ran his hands along her belly, and played with her belly ring.

"This is sexy, too. Maybe you could keep it covered when you're working?" he asked, leaning over her shoulder. She smiled, and he absorbed the sight of her full, round breasts, her pink nipples, and her lightly tanned areolas. He caressed upward and cupped one of them.

"That belly ring helps me get the tips."

He widened his eyes and pulled her tighter against him, while still cupping her breast. "A hell of a lot more than this belly ring is what gets you those tips."

She chuckled and then turned onto her side and looked at the painting.

He continued to caress her as they stared at the unfinished painting. "Are you going to finish this?" he asked.

"I'm not sure. I don't even know why I started it."

"Did you see the picture somewhere? Does it remind you of something?"

"The Tuscan sun? The view?"

"Yeah, maybe you saw it before somewhere and it stuck in your mind."

"I saw it before in books and online. When I was little, when my sister and I were close, we used to pretend that one day we would escape to a beautiful place, a home of our own on a vineyard, or in the country and out of Chicago. I guess when we both saw that beautiful Tuscan sun, we fell in love with it. It was like a fantasy of ours. But I was like eleven and she was nine and things with our parents got worse."

"You took care of her?" Billy asked.

"All we had was one another." She stared at the painting remembering her childhood. Billy caressed her belly, and snuggled up against her back. "I can remember her crying a lot. I just couldn't seem to keep her happy."

"Well, that's not an easy thing to do. If your parents were fighting a lot and finances were so bad, I'm sure both you and your sister felt it."

"Oh, we felt it all right. Especially when we went to school and our clothes were too tight and short, our hair a mess and we didn't have any of the things other little girls had." She tilted her head up, feeling the tears in her eyes.

"I didn't even have a Barbie doll, Billy. I didn't have any doll, or a stuffed bear I could snuggle with at night to keep my mind off of the problems and just be a kid." She snorted. "Can you believe that? Out of all the different things I could have used, even a damn hug once in a while, I remember not having a bear to cuddle with. My poor sister was younger and in even worse emotional turmoil. God."

"Hey, there's nothing wrong with what you just said. You know our parents didn't have a lot of money, but they did provide for us, take care of us, and sacrifice for us so we could succeed in life. I actually had a stuffed monkey I liked, a lot. Chester is what I called him."

She chuckled as she held his arm tighter against her chest. She loved that they were talking like this and sharing experiences. It made her feel even closer to him.

"How did you and your sister drift apart?" he asked her. She hesitated a moment as she thought about his question.

"I kept that dream of escaping, having a better life, and not allowing my parents to suck the life out of me. Annette didn't. By the time she finished middle school and went to high school, she'd already tried drugs, had sex, and was talking about running away. I tried to talk her out of it, but then she showed up at home less, snuck out at night, and I had my own problems."

"Problems?" he asked.

She turned to look up at him. "I was taking care of the small house and doing the grocery shopping, or else we would have starved to death. I paid the bills and cared for my mom when she drank too much. After she died, my father's business went downhill."

"What did he do for a living?"

"He had a small construction company. That's where I learned how to make a lot of things. I had to go there after school a lot because my mom was never around. I would get bored and would watch the carpenters working and they would teach me how to do things, especially when my dad was talking business, or trying to get a bill collector off his back. My dad tried to keep things from us about the relationship with my mom, but I heard them arguing at night. She cheated on him. A lot. Then she started over drinking and got sick. My dad was struggling to keep the house and to maintain his sanity and then he got hurt on the job."

"Oh man, what happened?"

"At that point Annette was screwing around and left home. My dad fell on one of his construction sites along with three other workers, and he was investigated. It turned out he wasn't operating the company the way he should have been. He got closed down, and even though he could have fixed the problems, he was at his wit's end. He was nasty, verbally abusive, and I was sixteen and taking care of a cripple, working to pay the bills for the house, and he wasn't budging. He was so depressed when my mom died, and then after the accident, there was no getting better. Every day his illness got worse, until one day, I walked into his room to wake him up, and he had died in his sleep."

Billy squeezed her tighter. "I'm so sorry you had to go through all of that. What did you do next?"

"I sold off everything. Didn't make a dime because money was owed on the house, and I focused and getting my life back. I finished school, paid off the bills, and then went to college."

"That's amazing, Michaela. You're very brave and very strong," Jake said as he joined them on the bed. Hal was there, too, now.

She looked toward the painting.

"I had a great job in Chicago in a corporate construction firm. I made smart investments and had a nice portfolio. Then I started to think about family more and more. You know being alone all the time on the holidays while all my friends and coworkers were with family grew old and depressing. So I decided to give Annette one more chance at keeping us a family. I decided I would try and if she declined, then I would take that trip to Tuscany on my own."

"It's not your fault that things didn't work out. You tried, and nearly died doing that," Jake told her.

"I know. But sometimes I feel guilty for a lot of things."

Billy caressed her cheek and turned her toward him. "Guilty for what? You went above and beyond what any child or person should have to in that situation."

"I watched my sister die after she told me she never wanted to see me again and that I was dead to her. I felt so hollow inside. I honestly don't know why I turned to the left instead of the right. Most people would have turned to the right. Even the doctors said it was amazing."

"You weren't meant to die. You were meant to do more. Can't you see that?"

She shook her head. "I couldn't see that because I felt so hollow, so estranged from everything and everyone, including emotions for so long. It's taken so much for me to let the three of you into my heart. And I'm afraid to hold on too tight, and that it might scare you away."

"Never. You could never scare us away. This was meant to be, Michaela. We're meant to be," Jake told her and then leaned over and kissed her cheek.

She smiled.

"How about we get something to eat?" Hal asked.

"That sounds great. I'm starving."

"So am I, but you are on the menu for dessert. Now come on." Hal lifted her up and began to carry her from the room.

"Wait, I need to get dressed."

"What for?"

"Well, you three are dressed in pants at least. Can't I put something on?"

Hal shook his head. "Nope. I want these accessible as we eat so I can suck on you in between." He leaned down and licked her nipple, pulling it between his teeth.

"You better give me something to wear or there won't be any nipple sucking allowed."

He paused. "Are you challenging me?" Hal asked. Billy chuckled at their little banter. Hal would win, but Michaela sure looked up for the challenge.

"What if I am, Hollywood?" she asked.

He widened his eyes. "That's one spanking coming up after dinner." He kept walking and Michaela gasped. "Spanking? Spanking? Is he serious?" she asked Jake and Billy over her shoulder.

Billy and Jake laughed and also looked forward to that spanking even more than their bellies looked forward to that BBQ chicken.

* * * *

Hal could see how uncomfortable Michaela was with her nudity. She kept one arm crossed over her breasts and her legs crossed. He pulled the T-shirt from the counter and passed it to her. "Here, put this on."

Her eyes widened.

"Really? It's not against your rules?" she asked, pulling the T-shirt on very quickly. Then she looked down at the firehouse logo. "Engine 19. Nice. Huge on me, but nice." She closed her eyes and inhaled the scent that brought a smile to Hal's face.

"Stand up, let me see what you look like in it?" Billy said, and she rose from the table, spreading her arms wide. The T-shirt was practically to her knees. Jake chuckled. "I'll get you a really nice sheriff's department one for you to wear." He took the last bite of chicken and winked at her.

"I think she looks fucking hot." Hal pulled her into his arms and immediately placed his hand under the T-shirt and over her ass.

"I bet you say this to all the women you seduce. What, do you have a box full of these T-shirts on your truck?" she teased.

Hal got serious. "This is my T-shirt. I've never let any woman wear my T-shirt."

She ran her hands up and down his chest and then cupped his cheeks. "Really, Hollywood? Why do I find this hard to believe?"

He squeezed her tighter.

"It's true. Ask my brothers. Maybe we gave away brand-new ones, but never ones we wore," he told her.

"Why not?" she asked, holding his gaze.

He pressed her back and over the kitchen table between Jake and Billy's plates.

As he leaned down closer to her lips, he used his hand to glide between her thighs and touch her pussy. "Too intimate of a gesture." He kissed her deeply, and then pressed his fingers up into her cunt.

Michaela surprised him as she lifted her thighs up and against his waist. Giving his fingers better access to her pussy and some leverage.

He stroked her cunt while he kissed her deeply, as his brothers commented.

"Well, we did agree that Michaela would be dessert tonight," Billy stated.

"Give us some room, Hal, you know how we love to share," Jake added.

Michaela moaned as Hal maneuvered a finger to her anus and pressed up into her. He was pumping fingers into her ass and pussy while Jake and Billy pushed up her T-shirt and began feasting on her breasts.

I could get real used to this. Coming home every night to Michaela, spread out on the dinner table like a feast for her men. She's absolutely perfect.

Chapter 7

"So you'll keep me abreast of any updates?" Jake asked Alonso as he spoke to him over the phone in the sheriff's department.

"Of course. I care a lot for Michaela, and just want her to be safe and happy. She doesn't need this type of danger."

"I should say not, Alonso. I have to tell you, from what you explained that your department and the Feds have so far, it's like this Solomon is after something specific from Michaela."

"I know, Jake. I'm thinking the same thing. I'm wondering why he hasn't left the country."

"I can't figure it out either. You said that the Feds had a lead on the tracker Solomon hired? What happened to that?"

Alonso was silent a moment. "They lost sight of him, but they also discovered that Dipero was in the same area."

"What? Why didn't the Feds grab him?"

"They don't have enough evidence to prove that Dipero killed Annette and shot Michaela. They're trying to figure out who hired Dipero to kill Solomon. And obviously, they believe it to be someone of importance or they wouldn't be giving this case a second glance."

"Oh shit. Could it be that they just want to get rid of Michaela because she's the only one who can identify the hit man and the fact that he was there at the apartment and shot both her sister and her?"

"Think about it, Jake. The Feds are involved. They had the gunman, the one who killed Annette and shot Michaela, in their sights, and they didn't get the order to take him in."

"Is this some political bullshit? Some organized crime going on in the government?"

Alonso chuckled. "We'll just have to wait and see. You and your brothers do your part and protect Michaela. If these men find her, it won't end nicely. Plus, if she even thinks they're around Treasure Town, she'll take off just to protect the three of you and everyone else in that town that has made her feel welcome. She's that special and unselfish."

"We'll take care of her, Alonso. Be sure to keep me posted."

"Will do."

Jake hung up the phone and then leaned back in his chair. He missed Michaela, was worried about her even moreso now, and he couldn't leave today to meet her for lunch.

* * * *

"Mr. Carlucci is busy right now. Perhaps I could help you with something?" Carlucci's personal assistant told Clyde Duvall.

"Oh, I think that your boss is going to want to drop whatever it is he's doing and come to the phone to speak to me. Just let him know it has something to do with some extracurricular activities he's doing, and some recordings that could possibly be used to slander him publically and maybe kill his chances for reelection."

"Hold on a moment."

"No problem."

Clyde stared at the house as he sat on the corner. The little brunette was renovating the place all alone. It would be easy to nab her or just get what he needed from her. All he had to do was notify Solomon so he could go in there and demand the key to the security box.

"I hope this isn't one of your bullshit ideas of a joke, Clyde. You know I don't have the tolerance for that shit."

"Sir, of course it's not bullshit. I just needed to let your assistant know that this is a serious situation."

"Explain."

Clyde went on to explain about Solomon's plan to sabotage the reelection, the thumb drive with loads of information that could not only incriminate Carlucci, but also a few associates in the political arena.

"This woman has this thumb drive?"

"That is what Solomon believes. Unfortunately, the woman is none the wiser. Solomon thinks that the sister, his girlfriend that your man Dipero killed, placed the thumb drive in a safety box with password access. Since Solomon is sort of on the run from your hit man and the cops, this woman is going to have to get that password and get the thumb drive for us."

"So grab her and get me that thumb drive by tomorrow."

"Oh, no can do. Let's talk a little business, Carlucci. For one, I didn't have to call you up. I got paid, cash from Solomon to track this chick and to get her to him so he could nail you to the wall and gain back his freedom. I want some big pay here on this one. Oh, and I also want Dipero off my ass. He's been steps behind me, but if he comes in here killing this woman and making a mess, we're all going down, and I won't be the only one singing your name like a canary."

"Okay, calm down. My assistant will call off Dipero. But you have forty-eight hours to get me that thumb drive."

"Seventy-two hours. The sisters were estranged and this one may not cooperate or may not even know the password."

"Get it done, or Dipero will take everyone out and no one will even know about the security box and thumb drive."

Carlucci disconnected the call, and Clyde smiled as he watched the young woman head down the street from her house. She was one sexy piece of ass. He wouldn't mind keeping her close and bringing her back to New York to the security box. Hell, he might enjoy a little playtime with her. He started the engine and headed in the opposite direction of the woman.

Soon enough I'll get out of her what I came here for and Solomon will be clueless.

* * * *

Michaela was grabbing a coffee at Sullivan's when Serefina joined her.

She was such a nice woman, and so pretty and easy to talk to. She wound up joining her for lunch and talking about town and how she grew up there.

"So is Treasure Town growing on you yet?" Serefina asked.

"It is such a nice town, nestled between the islands like this. It's incredible."

"Have you ventured to the outskirts and into some of the adjoining towns yet?"

"Nope. Too busy trying to fix up the house. This is the first time I even had a chance to come into Sullivan's."

"Oh man, then we need to go shopping and I can give you a tour of all the hot spots. How do you like The Station?"

"It's nice. Burt and Jerome are so wonderful. I can't complain. I only work the two nights."

"I haven't taken on anything other than this job here at Sullivan's. I had some trouble a few months back, and well, I moved here, back home, to try and get control of my life."

"Sounds sort of like me."

"I hope not. I had a serial arsonist stalking me."

"Oh God, that's crazy."

"Sure was, but my men and the other locals in town all helped to save my life. It was wild, but I'm finally starting to feel safe again. Well, with the help of Ace, Bull, and Ice. I don't know where I would be without them and my family."

Michaela felt emotional. She didn't have a family, but she did have Billy, Hal, and Jake. She was learning to trust them and count on them, too. She smiled.

"Thinking about your men?" Serefina asked, and Michaela chuckled. She could feel her cheeks blush. "Hey, no need to feel embarrassed. I know exactly how you feel. I came here from North Carolina after I lost my boyfriend to a fire I was trapped in."

"Oh God, that's terrible. I'm so sorry."

"Thank you. I was badly off, and really depressed. My family insisted that I return home, and when I did, the last thing I expected was to fall in love with three men. I tell you, it was scary. Then of course there was the serial arsonist. Well, I'll tell the long story another time. I want to know more about you. Where did you live before here?"

Michaela explained about Chicago but left out all the drama from New York.

"Hey, it's okay if you need your privacy. Believe me I understand. To be honest, I think you're a really nice person. I'm also happy to see that Hollywood, Bear, and Jake finally found the perfect woman for them. They were pretty devastated when Lisa left them. At least that's what Ace told me."

"I don't know anything about a Lisa."

"Oh God, I probably shouldn't have said anything."

"No, it's okay. It's not like I'm naive and thought that they were never with anyone else. I guess I'm just shocked that I felt instantly jealous."

Serefina smiled. "I am so like that, too. Even when I was trying to ignore the attraction I felt for Ace, Ice, and Bull."

Michaela smiled. "I guess when you care about someone, jealousy is a side effect." They both chuckled.

"If it makes you feel better, I heard Lisa was a nasty, two-faced snob and no one thought she deserved those men. Not even their dad."

"Yes, that does make me feel better." She held her mug of coffee and smiled.

"So how about we make plans to go to that boutique I mentioned? I would love you to meet my friends Tasha, Mel, and Catalina. We're going to try and make some plans for a girls' night out next week."

"That sounds like fun. When do you want to go to the boutique? I work Friday and Saturday nights."

"Okay, how about on Thursday afternoon this week?"

"Great."

* * * *

"What do you mean she's not at home?" Jake asked Hal over the cell phone.

"I just got here and she isn't answering the door. Why are you freaking out?"

"Shit. Just see if you can find her in town. Look for her bike. Ask Ike if he knows where she went?"

"Okay, now you have me concerned, Jake. If you know something and you're not telling me…"

"I can't get into it now, but I just got off the phone with Alonso and the news isn't great. He thinks that these men are getting closer. The Feds seem to be onto something, and when agents saw Dipero and then Duvall, they didn't nab them."

"Why the hell not?" Hal asked, raising his voice.

"Alonso thinks there's more going on with that Solomon guy who was dating Michaela's sister. He's trying to pull the pieces together along with the detectives working the case. He asked that we watch over Michaela."

"Great, and she doesn't even have a cell phone. Why?"

"Because someone could track her. She's smart and she's trying to remain under the radar. Look for her, I'm leaving the department now, and I'll look, too. Maybe she went toward the shopping strip?"

"I'll check the boardwalk. It's only a few blocks away."

Hal disconnected the call and got into his truck. He headed toward the boardwalk, keeping an eye out for Michaela as well as her bike. Once he parked the car, he walked the main strip and came upon Sullivan's. Maybe Serefina had seen her? Just as he headed closer, he spotted Michaela's bike and her sitting at a table talking with Serefina. He pulled out his phone and texted Jake before entering.

"Hey, Hal, what a nice surprise," Serefina stated as he approached. She stood up and he greeted her with a kiss to her cheek.

"Need a drink?"

"Iced tea is fine," he told her as she walked away.

He pulled the chair closer to Michaela and leaned forward to kiss her hello. Their lips touched and instantly he felt relieved. He realized just how much he cared about her already. Heck, he was in love with her.

"Are you okay?" she asked him, placing her hand on his shoulder as he moved his arm over her chair behind her shoulders. He leaned closer.

"I was worried about you when I stopped by the house and you weren't there."

"I decided to grab another book about renovating bathrooms. I was considering removing the old tub and placing a pedestal tub or maybe a free-standing one in its place. There's really nothing to salvage in the master bathroom. Here, this is what I was thinking."

She pulled the book from the shopping bag and fingered through the pages. Hal stared at her, absorbing her perfume and the way he felt so content and happy being this close to her and just talking about the house, renovating, and sharing her ideas. It was a great feeling, even though only minutes ago he was freaking out that someone may have taken her or tried to hurt her. His heart was still racing. But as she ran her fingers along the pages, pointing out a combination of ideas, he had to smile.

"I think that one would look great. Plus that other tub right there may not even fit down the hallway. It is kind of narrow up there."

She looked at him and stared up into his eyes. It was a moment, a period of time that passed around them, but their focus and their energy was consumed by these moments their gazes were locked.

She smiled and then pulled her bottom lip between her teeth.

"I know. I feel it, too." He placed his hand against her cheek and drew her closer for a kiss. This time when their lips locked, he felt the connection so strong and deep in comparison to any other. It was as if they both realized the intensity of their emotions. Releasing her lips, he ran his fingers along her hair.

"I guess we have some measuring to do."

She smiled and her eyes lit up. "You're going to help me?"

"Of course I am. I came by to see you and spend some time with you. Want to head out now?"

"I'll just make this iced tea to go," Serefina stated, interrupting the conversation as she twirled around and headed back toward the bar.

Hal and Michaela laughed.

* * * *

The moment he parked his truck next to Hal's Jake felt a bit more relieved, but only after seeing Michaela safe and protected with Hal would he be able to move on with his day. As he closed his door, he saw them holding hands and heading toward him. She smiled when she saw him, and all the fear drained from his body.

"Hey, I thought you had a lot of work to do?" she asked and immediately walked up to him, stood up on tiptoes, and kissed him. He held her in his arms and squeezed her.

When she went to pull back, he didn't let her go.

"Jake?" she questioned him, so he released her and then placed his hands on his hips.

"We need to do something about this whole no cell phone thing. We were both looking for you and there was no way to contact you. I was thinking that maybe I could add one to our service plan."

She crossed her arms in front of her chest even though she held a bag in her hands.

"Okay, what's with you two? It's like you're trying to keep tabs on me, or don't trust me. Does this have something to do with your ex-girlfriend?"

Jake felt the tightness in his chest and Hal looked about ready to drop.

"Ex-girlfriend?" Jake asked her.

"Listen, you don't have to explain anything to me about your past, well, lovers, I guess. I just hope you know that I care about you guys a lot and I'm not her."

Hal placed his hands on her shoulders from behind.

"No, you're not her." He then stared at Jake.

"I need to get back to work. I just wanted to make sure that you were okay."

"Is something going on? Did you talk to Alonso? Did he have an update?" she asked him. He looked at Hal.

"Not really. But just hearing all the details of their process and the fact that the Feds had Dipero and Duvall in their sights and didn't arrest them, does make me a bit concerned."

"What? Oh God, did he say where they were seen?" she asked as she shivered and looked around them. Hal pulled her against his chest.

"No. But probably not around here. Alonso will call me in the next few days. Don't worry. It seemed to me that Alonso would give the heads-up immediately. I'll see you a little later baby, okay?" He leaned down and kissed her. She allowed Hal to wrap his arms around her from behind as Jake got into his truck. As he left, he saw them head toward the beach, and he wondered if Hal would tell her about Lisa? Maybe that would be a good thing, and she could understand their fears just as she shared her fears with them.

* * * *

Michaela looked out toward the beach and the ocean. The sun was so bright it made both the sand and the water glisten. There were so many people enjoying the day. She had been living in Treasure Town for a couple of months or so now, and hadn't even come down here to enjoy the beaches. Maybe this weekend, on Sunday she would.

She closed her eyes and breathed in the smells around her. The salt water, the smoke drifting from a small barbeque by the picnic area, roasted peanuts, buttery popcorn, and even some hot dogs being sold by vendors along the boardwalk. The food carts on wheels reminded her of Chicago and New York. But these carts were shiny stainless steel, and each had gorgeous, vibrant umbrellas in various colors.

"Don't tell me this is your first time down here by the beach?" Hal asked, standing behind her with his hands on her shoulders. He was massaging her muscles, his wide, masculine body wedged against her smaller frame. She felt feminine and secure with Hal so close.

She placed her hand over the top of her eyes to block out the sun as she looked at him.

He squinted his blue eyes, which nearly matched the ocean water, at her, trying to hold her gaze against the rays of the sun. She turned in his arms and wrapped her arms around his waist.

"It's not so condemnable. After all, I'm sharing the experience with you first." She winked.

She felt his palm move slowly up her waist. It grazed the side of her sensitive breast before he placed it against her cheek.

"You're sharing a lot of firsts with my brothers and me."

She gasped and began to lower her eyes and head as her cheeks burned, but he held her cheek in place and leaned forward to kiss her.

When they parted lips, he squeezed her to him. "I love being with you."

"I love being with you, too. I thought you had to work today."

"Oh, I do. My shift begins in a few hours."

She wanted to ask him about Lisa. She wondered if they showed up like this because they were insecure. She didn't think it was possible considering how sexy, mature, and perfect he and his brothers were.

"You came out of nowhere and just when my brothers and I needed you, Michaela." He stroked the frame of her face as if he were admiring every bit of her. It made her feel self-conscious, yet aroused.

"I could say the same for you, Billy and Jake. God, when I think about how Jake and I met." She chuckled.

Hal got serious and gripped her hip snugger, drawing her closer against his body.

"That was a serious situation, and you could have been hurt or worse. Realizing what we do now, about your past, about getting shot, it's surprising how you handled that guy in the sheriff's department."

She swallowed hard. "It had a lot to do with my frame of mind, my determination to never be a victim again, and well, Alonso's help training me."

"I'll admit he did a good job and taught you some incredible moves. That kind of makes me feel jealous," he confessed.

"Jealous?"

"He had to have touched you, held you in his arms to show you step by step what to do."

She nibbled her bottom lip. "I'll admit we spent a lot of time together, but we realized very quickly that we were meant to only be friends. I told you before. I never had a boyfriend, never dated, or even fooled around. My life revolved around work, getting to a point where I was more than financially stable, and then giving one last attempt to hold on to family. I could have lost it all. But I didn't. Now I'm not going to say that hearing about this Lisa woman, or even thinking about all your past lovers, doesn't burn me inside. But it is the past. You're here with me now, and I think it shows that I'm willing to take a chance with you, Billy, and Jake."

He smiled. "We may have had a lot of experience with women. Hell, I'm sure we have like eight to ten years on you, Michaela, but I can definitely see the difference here. With you, everything is different."

She tilted her head at him in question. "Different how?"

"In every way." He looked out over the beach and ocean. "I feel different when I wake up in the morning and all day long. I think of you constantly. I worry about you. I fear that we won't be able to keep you happy, or that we might disappoint you. I worry about a lot of things because when we're together it feels so right."

She felt his sincerity, as well as the underline of fear he seemed to have.

She ran her palms up and down his chest over the shirt he wore.

"Hal, I may not have the experience you do, but I've learned the hard way that people shouldn't be taken for granted. That every day is a gift, every moment someone touches your heart, shows compassion, or gives freely of themselves, that it's a blessing and a gift. I don't know what tomorrow may bring. I don't know what next month, next year may bring my way, but right now, standing here with you, remembering how you, me, Billy, and Jake made love and spent so much time with one another, means everything. I don't know what that woman did to the three of you to make you fearful that I could do the same thing."

He started to talk and she cut him off.

"No, Hal. I'm not upset with you for comparing. I hope in doing so, you three will see that I'm not her. I'm me. I may come with baggage, I may even have that damn bull's-eye on my forehead still, but I'm honest and I'm real. I just ask the same of the three of you. Honesty. Plain and simple."

He reached up and stroked her lips with his thumb. He held her gaze and Michaela could see the struggle in Hal's eyes.

"Billy, Jake, and I thought that Lisa was the one for us. She played the whole ménage thing well. It had been great for months."

He told her and she felt her chest tighten. So maybe she didn't need to hear about her. Maybe it was a bad idea to pretend to be so tough and understanding? She hadn't expected the hurt, the pain in her belly just thinking about drop-dead gorgeous Hal, and sexy, sweet Billy, and macho, authoritative Jake sharing another woman. Not her.

She swallowed hard as he trailed his thumb very gently down her throat and across her collarbone. That pain of insecurity in her belly just turned to fire in her heart.

"What went wrong?" she asked, sounding breathless to her own ears.

He looked as if he were biting the inside of his cheek. He looked away, over her shoulder in the distance as he spoke. As if recalling it still hurt.

"She wanted more people in our bed."

She felt her body jerk in response. "Excuse me?"

He looked back down at her, still holding her firmly, still caressing her throat, her collarbone so intimately and softly even though his eyes were filled with fury and pain.

"She wanted more people in our bed. She wanted a fucking orgy, not a real committed ménage. Lisa was high class, wealthy, a snob in many aspects. The more we got to see her true colors, the more we drifted apart."

"What made you finally break things off?"

He stopped caressing her neck and stared at her as if he were uncertain he should tell her.

She reached up and laid her palm against his cheek.

"If you can't tell me, I'll understand. I mean if it hurts too much."

He took a deep breath and released it. "At first, it was because she cheated on us with two other guys."

"No."

"Yes."

"Stupid bitch."

Hal blinked his eyes, shocked at her response, and she saw the small smile appear and disappear quickly.

He pulled her closer and kissed her forehead. She hugged him tight.

His lips moved over her neck to her ear.

"No one knows what else she did, Michaela. No one."

She felt on edge. What more could this woman have done to them to make them feel such pain and to cut themselves off from any other relationship until now?

"Hal?" she whispered against his chest and shoulder. He held her closely. One hand was over her hip and ass and one flush against her lower back.

"She was pregnant with our baby. She didn't tell us and then she aborted it."

Michaela's eyes filled up with tears. These men were noble men, good men, who would have cared for that baby even if they didn't care for its mother. It was obvious that Lisa had issues. But to see how her decision had affected Hal, and more than likely Jake and Billy the same way, she felt terrible. She stood on tiptoes and hugged his neck as he ran his hands along her curves.

"I'm so sorry, Hal. You and your brothers must have been furious and felt betrayed."

"She said it was her body and she didn't want a child to ruin her figure and her social life. It was in those moments that we finally realized how wrong she was for us. We didn't know why we let it go on for so long. I guess it doesn't matter anymore."

She leaned back to look up into his eyes. She could see it still hurt to talk about it.

"Is this why you three spoke so much about trust?"

He nodded. "We have some fears of our own, as you probably figured out by now. Jake is already so overprotective of you. Billy is the same."

"And you?" she asked, giving him a smile.

He moved his hand up between them and caressed her breast.

"Hal." She looked around to be sure that no one saw his move.

He chuckled. "These are mine now. I can play with them whenever I want."

"Oh really?"

"Yes. In fact let's grab your bike and get back to your place. I think I need some cuddling time with you in your bed before I go to work."

She chuckled as he gripped her hand and pulled her along with him. She felt all giddy and excited inside. She was happy with Hal, Billy, and Jake. She wanted to hold on to this moment and sensation for as long as it lasted. Maybe everything would work out for the four of them after all?

* * * *

The moment the front door closed, Hal lifted Michaela up into his arms, causing her to drop her bag with the book in it. He didn't care, and neither did she as she ran her fingers through his hair and kissed him back. He pressed her against the wall at the bottom of the stairs and pulled from her mouth.

"Bedroom or right here?" he asked her.

"You're in charge."

"That I am." He reached for the hem of her blouse and tank pulling it up off of her and onto the floor. Her pretty pink polka-dot bra was a great contrast to her olive skin. "I love all these pretty bras you have, baby, but I prefer you naked."

He undid the clip, and the bra fell to the bend of her elbows as he cupped both breasts and feasted on them. He used his hips to secure her against the wall. She tilted her head back and thrust her hips and breasts forward.

He nipped one hard little nipple and then swirled his tongue around the areola as she moaned.

"Fuck. I need inside you now."

"Yes. Yes, now."

He pulled back and she grabbed at his T-shirt and pulled it up and over his head. He grabbed her hips and carried her upstairs as she licked and nibbled along his chest, shoulder, and neck. As her teeth pressed harder at a sensitive spot, he felt his cock thicken under his jeans.

He dropped her a few inches above the bed and grabbed for the zipper to her jean shorts, pulling them down roughly. Her eyes were glazed over with passion as he made quick work with his fingers to divest her then him of their clothing. But as he pushed down his pants, stepped out of them, and bent over, Michaela slid off the bed to the floor and reached for his balls and cock.

"Oh, sweet mother, don't. Please, Michaela, I can't."

She looked up at him with such a heated aroused expression. Their little inexperienced minx was looking to explore him.

"I want to taste you. Please you." She pressed her cheek against his cock as she stroked it. He reached down and ran his hands through her hair as he held her gaze.

"You do please me. More than anything in my life, ever."

She smiled softly and then opened her mouth and pulled his cock between her lips.

Hal couldn't hold back the moan or the fire that burned inside of him.

"Fuck, baby, that mouth of yours is incredible." He held her face and hand as she bobbed her head slowly up and down on his shaft.

He was trying so hard not to come inside of her mouth. He needed to possess her, fuck her deeply, and conquer these fears and insecurities he had after talking about Lisa.

When Michaela cupped his balls and rolled them around in the palm of her delicate hand as she sucked his cock, he grunted.

"Enough." He pulled from her mouth.

She gasped and squealed when he reached down, lifted her up by her hips, and brought her back onto the bed.

"Fuck, I can't hold back. You're too much." He aligned his cock with her pussy and thrust deeply into her cunt.

Michaela grabbed onto his shoulders. He felt her climbing his body, crawling, grabbing at him to get his cock to penetrate deeper. He knew in that moment that she was feeling as wild and needy as he was.

"Mine, all fucking mine."

"Yes, harder, Hal, please I feel so needy."

"I know, baby. God, I know it's incredible."

He grabbed her hands and pushed them above her head. He locked her wrists in place with one hand and then lifted up to cup one breast as he rotated and thrust his hips against her.

In and out he stroked her deeply, moving faster and faster.

She was shaking her head side to side at his relentless strokes. Then he felt her pussy muscles tighten. Her eyes closed and she screamed her release, lubricating his cock even more. He pulled out and thrust back in, releasing her wrists so he could grab her hips and get deeper, as deep as he could go so he could mark her forever.

"Michaela!" He roared her name and exploded inside of her.

They lay there together, panting, and she reached up and pulled him down to hug her.

"I love you, baby. I don't care if that scares you or not. I honestly love you."

She was silent a moment. He felt unsure and almost fearful but then he felt her lips against his neck, next to his ear.

"You like to be the first at everything, don't you, Hal?"

He laughed and rolled her to his side so he could cuddle up next to her on the bed.

She smiled, her blue eyes glistening with unshed tears. "I love you, too."

* * * *

Michaela finished taking a shower, and she put on the Engine 19 T-shirt she'd just washed and dried this morning. Jake and Billy were going to be coming by later, they were stuck at work, and Hal left an hour ago. She didn't see any reason to start working on anything in the house now, and besides, she was feeling content and tired after making love to Hal all afternoon.

She lay down on the bed and closed her eyes, thinking about Hal as the sun began to set outside her window. It was quiet, and there was a nice breeze drifting passed the cream-colored curtains. It wasn't long before she fell asleep.

It seemed as though she had closed her eyes only moments ago, but now her room was dark, and something awoke her.

She began to sit up when a gloved hand fell over her mouth and a body straddled her waist.

"Be nice and quiet, little whore, and I won't cut you." Her eyes zeroed in on the sharp blade of a large knife, and then the masked man on top of her. He had brown eyes, he was big, but he didn't appear to be Solomon or the hit man.

"Are you going to cooperate?"

She nodded her head.

"Good girl." He looked down at her breasts. "I thought that boyfriend of yours would never leave. I guess if you were my woman, with tits like these, I wouldn't leave you too soon either."

He pressed a hand up to her breast and she damned the fact she didn't wear a bra. His eyes widened and she struggled to push him off of her until the blade poked into her collarbone. It pinched and she knew he cut her.

"I'll cut your fucking throat. I don't give a shit. Now listen to me and maybe you'll live a little longer. Are you going to scream or try to get away?" he asked, and she shook her head. "Good."

Slowly he uncovered her mouth and she swallowed hard, her throat dry from the fear running through her body.

"What do you want?"

"Ah, a few things. You see, I need that key your sister hid with you. If I don't get it, then this very bad man is going to come here and he's going to kill you for it."

"What key?" she asked.

She never expected him to strike her but he did. Right across the cheek and mouth. She felt the instant pain and cried out.

"Don't fuck with me." He gritted his teeth in a threatening manner.

"I swear I don't know what key you're talking about. My sister and I weren't close at all. I went to see her and she told me she wanted nothing to do with me."

"She left the key with you or at minimum the instructions as to where to find it. Solomon said so."

"Solomon? I don't even know Solomon, and never spoke with him before."

He struck her again, obviously not believing her.

"Stop it. Please stop hitting me. I don't know anything about a key. My sister didn't trust me with anything. She wanted nothing to do with me."

"You're fucking lying!" he yelled at her and then raised the knife up above his head, and then struck downward right above her shoulder. She screamed out thinking that he would stab her in the chest and kill her but the blade hit her skin on her shoulder, cutting it.

She didn't know what to do and thought she was going to die when suddenly she saw someone enter the doorway over his shoulder. Michaela shoved at the masked man's chest making him lift upward as someone hit him in the head with a thick piece of wood. Her eyes flashed to Ike, and then her neighbor was holding a gun to the masked man's head.

"Are you okay, Michaela?" Ike asked her, a scowl on his face, as he held the gun in a pointed position at her attacker.

She covered her face and cried as sirens filled the air.

"Don't worry, your men are on their way," Ike told her.

The masked man didn't move as Michaela sniffled and wiped away the tears as the pounding of footsteps could be heard from the bedroom.

"We're up here. The burglar is out cold!" Ike yelled as Jake and a few other deputies entered the room, guns drawn.

"Michaela?" he yelled out, returning his gun to his holster as the deputies looked at Ike and absorbed the scene.

"Baby, oh God, you're hurt. You're bleeding."

She was shaking profusely.

"I need an ambulance. Get the paramedic up here now," Jake ordered. She closed her eyes and covered her mouth with her hand.

"It's okay, baby. I've got you, and that man can't hurt you anymore," Jake stated with such an explosive look in his yes.

She locked gazes with him. Her voice was shaking as she spoke.

"That's not him. That's not the hit man, Dipero. This isn't over."

Chapter 8

Jake stood at the end of the bed in the emergency room with Billy, Hal, and Detective Buddy Landers. Jake had called him earlier in the day to discuss Michaela's situation. When the call came in over the radio that Ike reported a break-in, Buddy responded, as well as over a dozen other law enforcement officers Jake and his brothers were friends with. Treasure Town was that type of community.

Michaela gasped as the doctor worked on the stitches to the deep cut above her shoulder. Billy was holding her hand, and Hal was caressing her thigh as the doctor worked.

"You're doing great, Michaela. Just a few more. I want to be sure to do this right," the doctor stated and winked at her. Jake just stared straight-faced, filled with a combination of anger, fear, and the need to hold Michaela in his arms. It was overwhelming.

When they first arrived, he and his brothers were concerned as Michaela couldn't stop shaking. The bruising on her cheekbone and jaw were fierce, and as Michaela gave her description of the events and how the masked man attacked her, he grew more and more angry. The fear that hit him when the call came into the sheriff's department took ten years off his life. He had just finished up at work and was heading out of the office. He'd called Hal and Billy immediately.

He was grateful that Ike had taken his request to keep an eye on things at Michaela's place seriously. He explained the situation to Ike, and Ike was retired law enforcement from New York. Even in his sixties, the man could kick ass.

Ike didn't like that Michaela's lights remained off hours after Hal had left. But then he walked around the house and noticed the back door lock was broken as if an intruder entered. Then Ike described how he heard Michaela scream. He dialed 911 and grabbed the thick piece of solid wood left from the construction. He also had his revolver on him in an ankle holster.

Jake was grateful.

"Did you identify that guy yet? Is he another hit man?" Michaela asked as the doctor finished up.

"Okay. Keep this ice on that cheek of yours. Try icing it as often as you can at home to keep the swelling down," he told her.

She nodded but looked right at Jake.

"Thanks, Doc," Billy said. "We'll go over the instructions with you in a few minutes."

The doctor nodded and smiled. "I'll be out by the front desk getting together the painkiller prescriptions and her release papers. Then I'll come back."

They said thank you and he left the room.

"Jake? Did you identify that man who broke into my home?"

Jake kept his hands on his waist and one leaning on his holster. "There's no need for you to worry about that right now. I'm taking care of it." Jake stared at her. The bruises were terrible. She didn't deserve this shit.

She went to move and cringed.

The men all reacted with concern, including Jake as he stepped toward the bed. The nurse came in right at that moment carrying a tray.

"You're going to have to lie still for a little while until these kick in. They'll help with the pain," the nurse told Michaela as she handed her two pills and a cup of water.

"Will these knock me out? I can't take heavy pain medication. They make me sick."

"You can take these as the doctor recommended while you heal. Besides, if you pass out, you have four men in here who can carry you." The nurse smiled and winked before heading out of the room.

"Take them, Michaela," Jake ordered. He was in a bad state right now. It wouldn't take much more to throw him over the edge. He didn't want her to feel any more pain, so if the medication helped, then he would make sure that she took it.

"Michaela, they'll help numb the pain so we can get you home," Billy told her more calmly, as he caressed her thigh.

She looked at him after giving Jake a dirty look. "I don't want to go to sleep." She lowered her eyes to stare at her hands. Hal covered them.

"The doctor said that rest is good. You need to take it easy so that the stitches don't come out, and so you'll heal quickly."

She shook her head and Jake wondered what she wasn't telling them. But then the doctor came back in.

"Okay. Take those and I can release you from the hospital tonight."

"I don't want to go to sleep."

"Why not? Sleep is a good thing right now, young lady. You look exhausted. Anyone would be after such an ordeal. The painkillers will only make you feel drowsy. They'll help ease your mind, Michaela," he told her, and she stared at him.

"Ease my mind? Are you sure?"

He nodded his head.

"I don't want to sleep. When I close my eyes—"

The doctor patted her hand. "I understand. It will take some time to get those images out of your head. There are counselors you could speak to. They may be able to help."

She shook her head. "I'll think about it." She took the pills and drank the water after swallowing them.

"Sheriff, can I see you for a minute to go over some things?" the doctor asked, and they headed out to the hallway.

"What's going on?" Jake asked him.

"I think your girlfriend is afraid to fall asleep and remember the attack. From the details she gave, she was half-dressed in her bed when this man broke in. That's quite traumatic in itself. She may have nightmares, trouble sleeping, or experience any number of side effects."

"Like what?"

"Shaking, panic attacks, anxiety, and a bunch more. She's going to need a lot of reassurance and she shouldn't be left alone. Especially in her house."

"We're taking her to our place. My father is at her house now, cleaning things up and grabbing some things of hers."

"Good. You call me if you have any questions or concerns. She's a brave young woman who survived a lot in her life. More than her share from what I gather. Take good care of her."

"You bet, Doc. Thank you."

Before he walked back in to help his brothers and Michaela, he thought about what the doctor said. She was trying to be so strong, but really she was terrified. Even to go to sleep. She needed them, and he would be sure to provide all the comfort and safety she needed. If he could just put aside the fear he had in caring so much so soon. It was crazy, but he knew he was being cautious because of Lisa. Michaela wasn't Lisa though. So when would he let down that wall and let Michaela in?

* * * *

Solomon couldn't believe what happened. Clyde, that backstabbing son of a bitch, double-crossed him. He found Michaela, and he didn't contact him to let him know. Solomon walked around Michaela's bedroom, way after the police left and it cleared out. Thank God it was nighttime and he could hide in the shadows.

As he walked around searching for where she could have placed the key to the safety deposit box, he started losing his patience. The blood on the bed indicated that Clyde had gotten rough. He kind of felt bad for Michaela. But then again, how was he to be sure that

Annette and she hadn't planned this whole thing from the start. Maybe Annette fucked up and hadn't planned on dying. But the sister now had a safety deposit box key with a quarter of a million dollars in it, multiple thumb drives containing incriminating evidence on three major politicians, and illegal passports for him and Annette.

As he thought about Annette, he realized that she would have never double-crossed him. Perhaps she really hadn't expected her long-lost sister to show up at the wrong time. Hell, he didn't even know that Carlucci hired Dipero to kill him and get the money he owed. He wondered how Carlucci learned of the thumb drives. Then he remembered letting Clyde know. Clyde was going to use them himself. Son of a bitch.

Just then he heard footsteps and men talking. Solomon panicked and looked around the room for someplace to hide. He didn't even have a damn weapon. He hurried toward the small window, shoved it open, and began to try and climb out when strong hands grabbed onto him, pulling him backward onto the floor.

"Who are you?" the older man asked.

"Don't move, asshole. The cops are on their way," the other one said.

"I'm a friend of Michaela's."

"Really? Then why are you trying to escape through the window?"

"I was surprising her. I came in and saw the blood and the mess. I got scared."

"You should be scared. Very scared."

Solomon stared at the two older men and thought he could take them. But as he looked toward the doorway just as the one man closed up his cell phone, he jumped forward and the other man struck him in the face, knocking him backward onto his ass.

"Go ahead and try to move again, punk, and watch what happens to you."

"Good job, Burt. The cavalry is on their way."

"You got a hold of Jake, Jerome?"

The Jerome guy gave an evil smile. "Sure did."

Solomon knew he was screwed. But maybe being in police custody could keep him alive a little longer.

* * * *

"I need to go. You two take her to our place," Jake told Billy as they were helping Michaela into Hal's truck.

"What's going on?" Michaela asked, sounding groggy as Billy buckled her into the front seat between Hal and him.

"Nothing, baby. I'll see you soon." He kissed her and then eyed his two brothers who looked pissed off and concerned. "I'll call you," he whispered to Billy, squeezing his shoulder, before he and Buddy Landers then ran toward their police vehicles.

* * * *

Jake couldn't believe that this was happening. His father and Jerome went to Michaela's house to clean up the mess in the bedroom and by the back door, as well as to grab some of her clothing. He got the call that they caught an intruder. A man claiming to be her friend. He knew it had something to do with this hit man and the Clyde guy they'd caught tonight.

Clyde was still in the hospital unconscious from the hit by Ike, so questioning him was going to have to wait. Perhaps this new guy, the intruder Burt and Jerome caught, could be of assistance.

Alonso was on his way from New York and should arrive any time now. The sheriff called the department and asked them to contact his cell and send him to Michaela's.

But as he pulled up in front of the house, where multiple police cars were, he saw the unmarked police car that he didn't recognize.

Jake hurried into the house.

There were Jerome and Burt talking to a man dressed in suit pants, a dress shirt, and tie, wearing a badge and a gun, and taking notes. Two deputies had the suspect handcuffed.

"Sheriff McCurran?"

"That's me. Is this the asshole who broke in?" Jake asked as he reached out to shake Alonso's hand.

"Detective Alonso Aponte, NYPD, special crimes unit. Pleasure to meet you in person. Looks like you're having a hell of a night."

"Looks that way," Jake replied.

"How is Michaela? Your father and his friend were just giving me an update."

Jake was surprised by the jealous feeling he had with this guy asking about Michaela. He knew that she was close to Alonso and that he'd helped her get through the shooting and taught her self-defense. But he was jealous anyway.

"She's with my brothers. She had to get stitches. The guy who attacked her, Clyde Duvall, stabbed her shoulder after he smacked her around. She's all bruised up."

He watched Alonso's face turn red, and he ground his cheek.

"I want to see her. I'm going to need a hotel tonight, but tomorrow I'd like to see her. We'll talk more later," Alonso stated as he eyed the man the deputies were holding.

"What should we do with him now, Sheriff?" one deputy asked.

"Let's bring him back to the department. The detective and I will need to question him. Detective Landers here will assist, too."

Jake introduced Alonso to Buddy. They shook hands as the deputies walked the prisoner out.

"That guy is Solomon," Alonso stated, and Jake's eyes widened.

"That son of a bitch is the one who caused all this shit? That Clyde guy said that there was a key and a safety deposit box. That's what he was after when he attacked Michaela."

"We need to go over some updated information the Feds have. By the way, they should be here shortly. They're going to want to speak with Michaela. I'd like to get you, Detective Landers, and your team up to par with what's going on. We can head to your department now. Then we can make plans for me to talk with Michaela first thing in the morning. Does she have protection now where she's at?"

Again, Alonso mentioned seeing Michaela. That bothered Jake, too. He never felt so possessive over someone. To even think that Michaela could leave him and his brothers for this guy had his stomach churning. If these thoughts kept up, he would grind his teeth to the gumline.

"I have two deputies guarding the location. Plus my brothers, and she'll have me as soon as I can get back to her."

Alonso looked Jake over. There was something in his eyes, the protective vibe for Michaela that made Jake like the man. A little.

"Good. She's lucky to have the three of you. I guess we can head out."

As they started to leave, Alonso was looking around the place. "She did a great job fixing this place up. It just doesn't do it justice in the pictures she sent over the Internet."

Again, Jake felt that bit of jealousy and possessiveness over Michaela. She was sending pictures to this guy over the Internet? He swallowed his annoyance as he remembered what Lisa had done. First she suggested having other people join them in their bed, and then she went out and cheated on them with two other guys. Although he knew that Lisa really wasn't the woman he and his brothers thought she was, it still hurt to think about it. To know that what they felt and thought they had with her was meaningless to Lisa. To think she killed their baby for selfish reasons, and to hold on to the beauty of her body, and to continue to engage in sexual activity, irked him. It also played havoc on his professional skills. He thought he could spot a liar from a mile away. Someone unethical, immoral, and devious as well, but he hadn't, and he and his brothers suffered dearly for it.

The fear of something like that happening again, or not being able to identify the warning signs, bothered him. He knew deep down that

Michaela wasn't Lisa. But as he overanalyzed her relationship with Alonso, Alonso's concern for her, the Internet communication and pictures, and the danger she was in, he worried a lot. Could they be making another big mistake? Could he be letting his own desire and emotions blindside him again?

The thought made him feel like shit, and also like he was betraying the trust he asked Michaela for. She was giving them that trust even though her own experiences should have held her back from risking it all. He was being a hypocrite. So why was he feeling that wall grow a little thicker? What would it take?

He wondered as he made his way back to the sheriff's department, knowing that he could be away from her a hell of a lot longer than just a few more hours. That burned him inside, when all he could think about was holding her in his arms, making her feel safe, and saving her from any further harm. Billy and Hal would have to do that tonight. His job was to ensure her safety from afar, and help Alonso and the Feds end this nightmare. Then maybe he and his brothers could figure out if Michaela was really who they hoped she was and the woman they longed for to complete them.

Chapter 9

Billy and Hal watched Michaela with concern, listening to her moan in her sleep. It was killing them inside. But at least the painkillers were kicking in and she was sort of resting. She had fought falling asleep and kept saying that she was scared. It tore their hearts. They wouldn't leave her side. They knew that two deputies patrolled outside. They also knew that Solomon broke into her home tonight and was looking for the key to the safety deposit box that the first guy who hurt her was looking for. It seemed to Billy that this case, this terror, was coming to a head, and keeping Michaela safe now was going to take a combined effort. They already received numerous calls offering assistance from their friends. They would probably need them.

"What are we going to do about Jake?" Hal asked.

Billy looked at him over Michaela's shoulder as they lay on either side of her on the bed.

"I think he'll come around. He's in his investigative mode. He's just as angry and pissed off as we are for not being there to protect Michaela. We knew she was in danger. We were too absorbed in ourselves, and maybe subconsciously we were trying to hold back a little. You know, out of fear of this relationship failing."

"I know what you mean, Billy. But this is different. I recognized it as different the moment Michaela began to open up and trust us. Hell, making love to her made me feel as if I could see the world with an entirely new perspective. I know that sounds crazy, but it's true. She's special."

Billy smiled. He ran a finger along her hair. "I know. She's so very beautiful, and sweet."

"I told her about Lisa today."

Billy turned to look at him, surprised at his brother's words. He worried about her reaction. Hell, he worried that sharing their ultimate fear could make Michaela even more nervous or resistant. She could think that they were on the rebound, or they were desperate for a replacement. He didn't think any of those things. In fact, he knew the three of them had given up on finding the perfect woman to complete them. That was when Michaela came along.

"How did she react?"

"She was sincerely sympathetic. Hell, she felt badly for us, and she said that she wasn't Lisa and that the three of us needed to be sure we know that. I'll tell you one thing. I felt a hundred percent better explaining our fear to her. I think that's why I felt so terrible that I left her today. We had a beautiful afternoon together. If I could have called into work sick, I would have."

"That's great. I think it's perfect that we can each spend time alone with her like that as well as together. It's a good way to get to know her and have that individual relationship, too."

"That in itself is different than with Lisa. You remember she didn't really like having sex spontaneously unless we were all together or at least two of us were there," Hal added.

"Fuck yeah."

"I'll tell you something else. I never felt so turned on by a woman before. I mean, I can look into Michaela's blue eyes, and see so much emotion and such a connection to me that it's fucking scary. Deep, too," Hal added.

Billy smiled. "I know what you mean. I got her something today. It's in the other room. It has something to do with the story she told me about growing up. You know she didn't even have a teddy bear or a doll? That's just wrong." Billy leaned down and kissed her softly on her good cheek.

She moaned again, and Hal reached over to caress her hair.

"I think we should get some sleep. I have the feeling that Jake won't make it home tonight, and when these painkillers wear off, Michaela is going to resist taking more of them."

"You're right. Let's leave the one light on. I'll turn this one off."

Billy reached up and turned off the light. He snuggled next to Michaela, and Hal did the same on the other side.

Billy looked at her as she slept.

She was perfect for them, and after what happened today, he wasn't going to leave her ever again.

* * * *

Michaela opened her eyes. She didn't recognize where she was. She turned toward the right and saw all the blood on the bed, and a body. A man's body. She cried out and as she scooted back, in an attempt to get away from the dead body, her back slammed into something solid and sticky. She felt it on her back, against her spine. She turned quickly, and saw the other body, screaming in terror, she scrambled off the bed. The moment she hit the floor, the pain radiated over her shoulders and into her legs.

She looked around, and tried to push herself up off the rug when she saw the third body. Jake's face stared at her lifeless. She screamed again, and cried out.

"They're dead, and you're next."

She turned toward the doorway and saw the killer. Don Dipero the hit man holding the gun and pointing it at her chest. She felt her heart sink and knew it was the end just as he shot her, she jerked backward and cried out in pain.

* * * *

"Michaela! Michaela!" Hal called her name and she wouldn't respond. Billy was trying to keep her still, but she was throwing herself around. She fell to the floor off the bed as he tried to hold her. It was as if she were stuck in a nightmare.

Suddenly her eyes popped open. She was gasping for air, hyperventilating.

"Calm down, baby. You're safe. You're with us, and you're safe."

She darted her bulging eyes from Hal to Billy and then toward the doorway. There was Jake, looking exhausted and wearing his uniform pants and no shirt.

"Is she okay?" Jake asked.

"Baby, you were having a nightmare," Hal told her.

Billy reached for her shoulder to check the bandage. "Shit, you could have opened up the stitches."

She cried and then rolled toward Hal, hugging him as she straddled his waist. Hal held her tight, trying to be sure that she didn't bump the stitches any more then she already had.

"I've got you, baby. I've got you."

* * * *

Michaela couldn't comprehend what the hell just happened. Now that her mind was clearing, although still fuzzy, she realized that what Hal and Billy said was true. It was a nightmare, so vivid and real and obviously brought on by the damn medication.

"I'm not taking the painkillers. Do you hear me? I'm not taking them. I can't. I won't, Hal. You hear me? I'll take some damn ibuprofen."

Billy caressed her back and then her rear. That was when she realized she was only wearing a T-shirt and panties.

"It's going to be okay. Maybe if you take half a pill, it won't happen again and might take the edge off?" Billy suggested.

"No freaking way. I need my head clear."

She snuggled against Hal's neck and she kissed his skin. She was trembling when Jake sat down on the edge of the bed. Billy kept caressing her lower back.

She turned to look at him, and saw the exhaustion on his face, as well as something else. His eyes looked dull, and he wasn't touching her.

"We're going to have some company in a couple of hours."

"Company?" she asked.

"Some Federal agents, and Alonso, probably even Buddy and few of the detectives on our team. We did a lot overnight and it seems we need to ask you some questions."

She didn't like how he sounded. It was almost as if he thought she was guilty of something.

She started to sit up, and scrunched her eyes together. Billy and Hal helped her.

"Jake, you know that Michaela is not involved in anything," Billy stated.

Michaela stared at him. "I'll answer any questions I can. What did you find out? Why would they think I've done something illegal?"

"There's evidence that the Federal agents have gathered through the investigation. Solomon asked for an attorney. He's keeping his mouth shut. Right now he's on the way to a secure facility until the Feds can follow through with the entire legal process of questioning him. But they do have phone recordings between him and Clyde. Apparently he hired Clyde as a tracker to find you. Dipero isn't far behind. In fact, they believe him to be in the near vicinity."

She gasped as Billy and Hal started to ask questions. They were concerned.

"You should get dressed. We'll make something to eat and then be ready for them." Jake got up slowly and as if he was dragging from lack of energy. He looked emotionally distraught.

"Jake?"

He stood there, inches away from her, and stared at her face and then looked away. Why?

"Why won't you look at me? Do you think I'm a criminal? That I was somehow involved with my sister and a possible plan to rip off Solomon? I didn't do anything. I don't know a thing. How could you believe for one moment that I would be someone I'm not?"

He sat down on the edge of the bed and cupped her good cheek.

"Michaela, I'm sorry. I know that you're not a bad person. I believe that you had nothing to do with this entire fiasco. I'm just tired and confused, and I guess staying guarded is what I do best." He went to pull away and she grabbed his hand. The move hurt her shoulder but she didn't care. Thinking that Jake was putting up a wall from fear of the past was more painful.

"Jake. I'm not Lisa. I didn't lie about any of this. I didn't lie about caring for you. I didn't lie about anything. In fact, you, Billy, and Hal know more about me than anyone else. I'm scared, Jake. I don't want to die. I don't want to lose the three of you. I need you."

He pulled her gently into his arms and hugged her tight. "I'm sorry, baby. Please be patient with me. I'm only human."

She chuckled. "Are you sure? I thought you were a sheriff. Aren't sheriffs supposed to be tough as anything?"

Billy and Hal laughed.

"You better watch yourself, little lady. A spanking or two may be coming your way."

She felt her cheeks warm as Billy caressed his hand over her rear and Hal cupped her breast.

"I don't deserve any such thing. Besides, I'm injured and need you to take care of me. You can't spank an injured woman."

Jake reached down and ran a finger between her ass cheeks. "There's a lot of fun I can have with you. But you're right. You're injured and you need to heal." He stood up and she felt so very disappointed. But then as she tried to cross her arms and huff in response, she gasped.

All three men had scowls on their faces.

"Get her showered and dressed. I'll handle lunch."

He walked out and Billy came around to help her up and off of Hal.

He carried her to the bathroom and started the water in the large tub for a bath. She was hoping for a shower, and for Billy and Hal to join her, but no such luck. As she looked in the mirror, she cringed in shock.

"Oh God, no wonder why Jake couldn't look at me. This is terrible."

Hal wrapped his arms around her waist. "He wishes he could have gotten there sooner, just as I wish I hadn't gone to work and instead stayed with you in bed."

"It happened, Hal. There's nothing we can do about it now."

"You're safe with us. We're not leaving you again. Never," Billy stated and then leaned forward and kissed her. Hal hugged her tight and then both men gently removed her clothing before Hal placed her into the tub.

"Be sure not to wet the bandages. I'll go grab you some clothes." Hal told her.

Billy kneeled next to the tub.

"I can imagine more nights like this, Michaela. You soaking in the tub as I come home from work, missing you so."

"That would be nice, Billy. Minus the hit man, the bruises, the knife wound, and the Federal agents."

"Yes. Minus all of that. Instead, just the four of us, happy and making love."

She closed her eyes. "Sounds perfect."

His lips touched hers and she kissed him back, enjoying the moments of relaxation, security, and love between them, knowing that shortly, she would be the subject of an interrogation she wasn't looking forward to experiencing.

* * * *

Solomon felt scared and unsure even as the Federal agents followed the security vehicle to a local police department a few miles outside of town. As the car pulled alongside the back entrance to the building, they prepared to accompany the officers assigned to transporting Solomon into the building. The moment he emerged from the vehicle, he heard the squeal of tires and saw the van coming at them at a high speed. Immediately the officers pulled him down behind the car. With guns drawn and safety taken behind the patrol vehicles, the agents and officers dodged flying bullets as the officers secured Solomon and returned fire. Solomon thought this was it.

Oh God, I'm going to die. Carlucci is everywhere. The Federal agents and the officers fired repeatedly causing the van to crash into two parked patrol cars. Running toward the van as the perpetrators attempted to escape, more shots were fired. The officers tried to pull Solomon into the building as the bullets ricocheted of the car, and through the door. He felt the hit. Solomon cried out and tumbled to the ground. An officer covered him. He could hear yelling. Officers were hit. It was such an eerie feeling as a few extra shots rang out, and then there was silence. Solomon felt his heart racing. He saw all the chaos, the blood, the smoking vehicles, the injured officers and a thousand thoughts ran through his mind. He was frightened, but he was also pissed off. *If I'm going to die anyway, I might as well take the asshole with me.*

He watched as all the perpetrators were captured. He could also see some dead bodies where he now stood.

As the main Agent Thompson ran toward the officers and agents guarding Solomon, he saw the blood oozing from Solomon's arm.

"You were shot?" Thompson asked. The other men were all unharmed.

"They were going to kill me. I changed my mind. I don't need a lawyer. I'll talk to the detectives and to you guys. I'll tell you everything. But I want protection. Otherwise, I'm a dead man walking."

* * * *

The men had an open floor plan in their three-story home a few blocks from the beach. The kitchen and dining room were filled with about a dozen or so federal agents, detectives, and deputies. As Michaela slowly walked into the room, their chaotic chatter stopped. They were silent as they stared at her.

"Aw hell, sweetie, what did that asshole do to you?"

She turned to see Alonso as he gently pulled her into his arms and hugged her.

"I've had better days."

He gently cupped her good cheek and kept a hand at her waist as he looked over her injuries.

"I hope you were able to get a few shots in on the guy."

"Nope. The sharp knife he had halted me from antagonizing him. My self-defense instructor taught me well," she teased. He leaned forward and kissed her cheek.

"Michaela, we have a chair set up for you here," Jake interrupted, looking angry as usual. He held the top of a large cushioned chair that stood out of place from the kitchen and dining chairs made of wood. It was obvious that he wanted her to be comfortable so he'd pulled it in from the living room.

Then the introductions were made. Of course she wouldn't remember any of them.

When she sat down, Jake placed a hand on her shoulder and squeezed it gently before he took a seat beside her.

When Alonso took the seat on the opposite side of her, Billy and Hal were forced to stand behind her chair and out of sight.

"Michaela, Agent Reynolds, Agent Thompson, and Agent Robertson, have some updates for you. I'll let them explain," Alonso told her.

She looked toward the three agents he had directed her attention to when stating their names. One was tall and dark skinned with a fierce expression. The other was very pale looking, smiled kindly, and seemed more approachable. The whole good cop bad cop scenario came to mind. She reminded herself that she wasn't guilty of anything. The third agent remained quiet, and watched her, probably analyzed her eye movement and body language to see if she were lying. It gave her the chills.

"Last night, while you were at the hospital, Solomon broke into your home."

"What?" She turned to look at Jake who remained straight-faced. She then looked at Alonso, who gave her hand a pat. It didn't go unnoticed by Jake.

"He was apparently looking for a key. The one that Clyde Duvall was looking for when he attacked you. The sheriff's father and his friend were there gathering items for you when they walked in on him."

"Are Burt and Jerome okay?" she asked Jake, and he nodded. "They were able to restrain Solomon until my deputies and I arrived."

"In that time, Michaela, he refused to cooperate with our questions and he demanded a lawyer. We had to respect that right," Agent Thompson continued.

"So what happens now?" she asked.

"Well, when we were transporting Solomon to another department a few miles out of Treasure Town, there was an ambush. A van filled with men with guns tried to kill him. We fired back, causing the van to crash and were able to capture the perpetrators."

"Don't tell me that they were successful. Solomon could probably clear up this entire mess. He was the one who ran from the room. The one the hit man had come to kill."

"He was shot, Michaela. But it was only a flesh wound. It was enough of a scare to get him to drop the attorney thing and cooperate."

"Oh, thank God." She looked toward Jake and then toward Alonso.

Alonso covered her hand and looked her in the eyes. "Sweetie, without getting into too many details, there is a key, a safety deposit box, that contains items that could incriminate a few very powerful individuals," Alonso said.

"Men in political positions who would be destroyed by the information supposedly contained on thumb drives located in this security box," Agent Thompson told her. "Solomon swears by this. He was going to use the information to stay alive, and to blackmail these politicians. He tried to sell some of the info to a certain political figure. Once that politician got the information, he apparently was dissatisfied and wanted his money back or more info on a competitor."

Alonso held her hand.

"That was the day that you went to speak with your sister. She didn't know anything about this deal, from what evidence we gathered as well as from Solomon's sworn statement. But, he did ask her to keep the key in a secure location. He had no idea where she put it, but after some investigating, he found out about a security box, a key, and some password. We were able to locate the security box's location, but even with a warrant and the fact that we are investigating a murder, that box cannot be opened except by the owner or co-owner."

"But Annette is dead," Michaela whispered.

The agent held her gaze. "Your sister placed your name down as the co-owner of the box," Agent Thompson explained.

"Me?" She pointed to herself in shock.

"Yes. She also set up a second security box, too."

"So what does this mean? What do you need me to do? Sign something so you can open the box?"

"They're password protected. It's a double measure to ensure security," Alonso told her.

She looked at him and thought about what they were saying. "How the hell would I know a password Annette set up when we've been estranged for so many years?"

"Sweetie, she obviously thought that you could figure it out," Alonso said.

"Or she thought that it would never come down to this because she told me straight out she wanted nothing to do with me."

"She could have been trying to protect you. It's a possibility, but it was too late. Dipero showed up, shot her, and then you before going after Solomon," Alonso suggested.

She shook her head. "There's no way," she whispered, her voice cracking at the thought that perhaps her sister, after all they had experienced as children, was finally protecting her, the way Michaela had always protected Annette.

She placed her hands over her face and closed her eyes.

She felt Jake place his hand on her knee.

"Perhaps it would be best if you wrote down some things that you both liked or knew she liked? Perhaps a pet's name? A favorite doll?" Agent Thompson asked as he opened up a notepad. She uncovered her face and stared at him.

Her entire mind went blank. She shook her head. "I can't even think of anything."

They all looked so bleak. Like without this information, they had no case, just hearsay from some lowlife like Solomon.

"You need to try, Michaela. Without those thumb drives, we don't have a strong enough case to bring these politicians and the hit man down," Agent Reynolds added. He was the uptight one.

She felt her stomach ache.

"I'll need some time. Is there a certain number of letters to the password?" she asked.

"We'll see if we can at least get that for you. We'll have someone on standby who can get in touch with the bank's administrator assigned to the case," Thompson told her.

They explained more about the investigation and she understood the seriousness of it. She remembered the stack of items and a box of her sister's that Annette's landlord gave her. Michaela never looked at it. She was too distraught.

She looked at Jake as the agents began to get up and leave. Jake accompanied them out of the room and then she stood up as Billy and Hal came over to her.

"That was a lot to take in. You'll figure it out. We'll help you," Hal said.

"Michaela?" Alonso approached, so Hal and Billy gave them some space.

He took her hand and then placed his fingers under her chin. "Those are some nasty bruises. Have you been icing them?"

"Not like she should be," Jake stated, returning, with his arms crossed in front of his chest.

Alonso looked at him and then back at Michaela. "Let's sit down and talk. It's been a while." He escorted her into the living room where they sat together on the couch.

She glanced over her shoulder at her three lovers who looked jealous and pissed off. She didn't want them to think that she had something more with Alonso than friendship.

"You guys can come sit, too," she offered.

"We'll give you a few minutes to catch up," Hal said and then walked further into the kitchen. By the floor plan all three men could hear their conversation and keep an eye on her. She smiled at Alonso.

"They care for you a lot," he said and smiled.

"I care for them a lot."

"I can tell. I'm happy for you, Michaela."

She smiled and nodded her head.

"I know that all of this had been a lot to take in. From our time together, I learned of your fears, your distrust, and your feelings of betrayal from your sister and family. Hearing all this information now, and learning about the security box and password, perhaps in her own way she was trying to give back to you the protection and security you gave to her all those years as you protected her."

"By nearly getting me killed? By making it so that these criminal politicians and crazy hit men are looking to end my life so that I can't open that box and incriminate them?"

"They don't know about the password. They only know that Solomon had access to the thumb drives, and that he hired Clyde to find you because Solomon told Clyde about the thumb drives and that Annette left the key with you."

"Alonso, I won't be able to figure out the password. I don't even know who my sister was these past many years."

He placed his hand on her knee. "I think you'll figure it out. Try thinking about the times you shared together. The similar things you enjoyed. Any guess whatsoever and you contact me and the agents."

"Okay. I'll try."

He reached up and cupped her cheek. "I'll be in touch." He leaned forward and kissed her cheek before he got up, said good-bye to the men, and then left the house.

Billy, Hal, and Jake walked into the living room.

"He cares a lot about you," Hal said.

She smiled. "We went through a lot together. He's a good person."

"I think he touches you too much, and I don't care for the way he calls you sweetie," Jake snapped.

"Come here, Jake," she told him and he stepped closer. She patted the couch and the seat beside her. Jake sat down.

She looked at him. "I care for you, Hal, and Billy a lot." She clenched her teeth and climbed up on top of his lap, straddling him.

He cursed under his breath and reprimanded her for moving around like that with the stitches. But he held her by her hips.

She placed her hands on his shoulder. "I don't have feelings like that for Alonso. Don't be jealous. Don't look for reasons to keep pushing me away. I was the one with trust issues, abandonment issues, insecurities, and so on. I need you Jake. I need you so much right now as more than just a lover, a man I lust for, but as a friend, a companion, a support network, and my man. Can you find it in your heart to be there for me and trust me as I trust you?"

He swallowed hard. Then he cupped her cheek drawing her closer to his face. His blue eyes looked so intense, but they were shiny, not dull, and filled with excitement and life.

"Of course I'm here for you, baby. I love you." He kissed her softly on the lips, and soon that kiss grew deeper. He stroked her breasts, ran his hands long her back, and cupped her ass.

Their lips parted and they were forehead to forehead.

"I love you, too."

"What about us?" Hal asked, as he and Billy joined them on either side of Jake.

She smiled as she glanced at Hal and then at Billy.

"I love you both, too."

"And we love you."

They all smiled.

"So isn't this when you carry me upstairs and make wild passionate love to me on your king-size bed?" she asked, wiggling her eyebrows at them.

Heat and hunger passed over their eyes, and Jake squeezed her hips. "You have stitches and bruises," he reminded her.

"I want to. I want all three of you."

Jake looked at Billy and Hal. "Go lock the top lock on the door. This is going to take some time."

He stood up from the couch with ease and grace and headed toward the staircase.

Michaela hugged him tight, feeling the slight twinge of ache in her shoulder, but her desire to make love to her men was stronger.

Jake set her feet down and removed her clothing slowly. Especially her shirt, as they had to stretch the material to expand over the bandage.

Once she was naked, she helped him undress, and Billy and Hal got things ready.

Jake gently pressed her back until her legs hit the bedside.

"Nice and slow, Michaela. I'm in charge now."

She sat down on the bed. He softly pressed her back and then used his palms to spread her thighs.

She moaned as her pussy automatically wept with need, and her nipples hardened.

Billy and Hal were on either side of her, and began to explore her breasts with their mouths as Jake explored her pussy.

Jake's first touch to her cunt sent her moaning and thrusting upward. His thick, hard finger stroked between her pussy lips, sliding against the cream that soaked her there. He held her gaze, her chin to her chest, and she was mesmerized by the desire and hunger in his eyes.

"I can't wait to taste you. Your pretty pink pussy is calling me." He pressed a finger up into her and began to stroke her cunt. She moaned and Billy and Hal tongued her nipples, making the protruding flesh harden into pebble-like forms.

Then Jake pulled his finger from her pussy and stroked the cream to her anus. She shivered with anticipation, knowing she loved the feeling of two cocks inside of her, and that she would always love that with her men.

"Oh, Jake."

He pressed his mouth to her pussy lips as he pressed his finger to her anus. In and out he stroked both holes, pulling more and more desire from her body and numbing her mind of any pain from her shoulder or her cheek.

He was resilient and thorough, thrusting, sucking, nibbling, and stroking her until she tightened and released more cream.

"Please, Jake. Please," she begged him. He pulled mouth and finger form her body, stood up straighter, and gripped her ass cheeks as he aligned his cock with her pussy.

"Nice and easy," he told her as Billy and Hal each cupped a breast and kissed her shoulders around the bandages.

"Jake." She raised her voice in demand as he entered her in one smooth stroke. His cock felt so thick and hard, she wiggled, nearly forgetting about her pain in the shoulder.

Over and over again Jake made love to her, thrusting, rotating his hips, trying to ease the ache they both felt.

"I love you, Michaela," he said through clenched teeth as he exploded inside of her.

Michaela reached up and ran her palm up and down the thick pectoral muscles on his chest.

"I love you, too, Jake," she whispered.

Jake eased out of her, and Billy took his place.

* * * *

Billy eased his way between Michaela's thighs with a soaring heart filled with joy and love. He never thought he would feel like this but he did.

He massaged her thighs and held her gaze as he slowly pushed his cock into her tight pussy.

"You sure you're up for this."

She gasped and nodded with her head tilted back, her breasts pushed forward, and her delicious body rose in offering. The sight of Hal's large hand cupping and massaging her breast and pointing her nipple upward before Jake licked it, made Billy harder. He increased his thrusts and absorbed the feeling of togetherness with his brothers and Michaela. This was the sensation they longed for. Michaela was their missing link.

"Faster, Billy, please. I'm okay. Please," she begged. He reached for her hips as Hal and Jake pinched and played with her breasts. Thrusting into her, rocking his hips harder and faster as she moaned and then cried out, sending him over the edge. Billy called her name as he came inside of her, and then lowered to her chest. Hal and Jake moved as he kissed her on the mouth and then trailed kisses along her breasts and belly.

"I love you," he whispered, and she reached up and placed her hand against his cheek. "I love you, too." He turned his face and kissed her palm.

* * * *

Billy eased out of the way and Hal took his place. Hal lowered to his knees, used his palms to spread Michaela's thighs, and then thrust a finger up into her cunt.

She moaned and turned her head side to side as he continued to arouse her. After pulling the tube of lube from the side of the bed he had placed there, he squeezed some onto his other finger and brought it to her anus.

"I love this ass and this pussy. I know you're too sore right now to take us all at once. But I want to play a little, and help you to relax and forget about anything but us right now. Okay?" He stroked the wet finger over her anus. She nodded her head and then gasped.

Back and forth he glided his finger against her anus but didn't push up into her. He used his other finger to stroke her cunt and she began to wiggle and push against both digits.

He locked gazes with her from below. She looked so sexy. Her thighs spread wide over the edge of the bed. Billy held one back and Jake held the other. She was panting, her face was flushed, and her pupils nearly dilated from him teasing her like this. His cock grew harder, thicker with anticipation.

"Please, Hal. I need it."

"Need what, baby, tell me," he asked as he continued to glide his lubricated finger back and forth over her anus barely applying pressure but enough to stimulate her and make her cunt release tiny spasms of more cream. She was dripping wet.

"You, inside of me. Stop teasing me."

He stroked his finger and she pressed her ass down trying to make his finger enter her.

"You like it when one of us fucks you in the ass, baby?"

"Yes. Yes, do it. Do it," she begged.

"Damn, Hal," Jake whispered. Both he and Billy looked equally aroused as they held her thighs wide, looked over to watch what he was doing, and kissed her thighs and knees.

"You want this?" he asked, and pressed his finger gently over her puckered hole and slightly into it.

"Yes, damn you. Please, Hal. Oh!" she screamed as her pussy exploded.

Hal pulled his fingers from her cunt and ass and squeezed the lube onto her anus. He aligned his cock with her puckered hole and blew warm air against her pussy. She shivered and shook, and growled with need. Slowly, he pushed through the tight rings of her ass, as both Jake and Billy pressed fingers over her cunt.

Michaela screamed again as she wiggled and exploded again.

"Fucking beautiful," Billy whispered.

"She sure as hell is," Jake said, leaning back and kissing Michaela. Hal continued to thrust his cock into her ass as Billy played with her pussy. He pressed a finger up into her cunt and Michaela moaned and plead for mercy.

Hal locked gazes with her from above.

"You feel incredible, Michaela. You should see how your tight, sexy ass is pulling my cock in deeper. You want it deeper, baby?"

"Yes. Yes, please, I think I'm coming again. I feel so tight."

Hal pulled out and then thrust back into her ass as Billy continued to stroke her cunt.

"Oh God. Oh God," she repeated. Hal thrust one more time as Michaela shook and screamed another release, this time with a guttural cry of pleasure that had Hal shooting his load and gasping for air.

"Holy shit," Billy said aloud as he pulled his finger from her pussy and leaned down to kiss her lips. They eased her thighs down as Hal slowly pulled from her ass. He kissed her belly, then licked over the belly ring and up to her mouth. She grabbed a hold of his hair and pulled him closer to kiss her deeper.

"I love you," she told him.

"I love you, too," he replied.

They lay together on the bed, recuperating from their lovemaking session when Michaela looked at Jake.

"As much as I would love to stay here like this forever, we have some work to do."

"Work to do?" he asked as Billy and Hal sat up, leaning on their elbows and caressing her thighs.

She smiled. "We need to go to my place. There's a box of Annette's things, and maybe something might trigger a memory of the possible password. I didn't open it. I just stuck it up in the attic."

"Why didn't you mention this earlier to Alonso and the Feds?" Jake asked.

She cupped his cheek. "I don't need a bunch of strangers around, putting pressure on me, making me nervous right now. I need men I trust. The safety and security that the three of you can provide for me as you help me think things through. We're a team now, remember? I can only get through this with the three of you by my side."

Jake smiled. "Did I tell you how much I love you?"

"You can tell me every day for the rest of our lives, Jake. It will never grow old."

Chapter 10

Michaela was feeling frustrated as she sat on the bed in her bedroom, completely baffled. She had texted Alonso several times with various suggestions as passwords. None of them worked. She had her sister's items scattered around the floor in front of her and on the bed. She was so relieved that Burt and Jerome, as well as Serefina and her mother, came over to clean up the bedroom. No one would ever know that she was attacked in here.

"Hey, do you need to take a break?" Billy asked, leaning inside the doorway. He had left a little while ago, saying he forgot something at their house. Jake and Hal remained downstairs.

She placed the wine ornament back into the small box wondering what that meant. She had been analyzing every item and trying to see if its name or something similar had nine letters. The Feds said a nine-letter-word password. There could be a million possibilities.

"I would love one."

"Good. Before I come in, I just wanted you to know that I picked something up the other day for you. I don't know if this will make things worse, or if it's not the right time, but, well, I'll just give it to you anyway."

She looked at him, wondering what he was talking about, when he reached back behind the wall in the hallway and returned holding a huge, four-foot-high, fluffy brown bear with a great big pink bow.

"Oh my God!" she squealed, moving quickly toward the edge of the bed as he set it on the floor.

"For me?" she asked as Jake and Hal entered the bedroom next. The tears streamed down her cheeks. She hugged Billy and then she hugged the bear. He had truly listened to her. They all did when she explained about having nothing as a child. Not a doll, a stuffed bear, nothing.

She hugged the bear, cringing that her shoulder ached, but she was suddenly filled with such magical joy it shocked her. She stared at the bear, remembering as a child how she wished she had one to cuddle with at night. Especially when her and Annette cuddled as their parents fought. She closed her eyes, the emotion overwhelming as she held her hand over her chest.

"Aw, baby. If it's too much, I'll take it away," Billy said, reaching for it and moving it toward the wall.

"Don't you dare, Billy McCurran. I love it. I'll keep it forever." She reached for his hand and he pulled her into his arms. He kissed her deeply and then Jake and Hal kissed her next.

Jake looked at the bed and cleared off some of the items. "This is a lot to look at," he said as she lay on the bed, facing the wall she had finished painting and all the items from her sister's box. The big bear sat right next to it and she stared at it all.

Billy took off his shoes and got onto the bed with her. She snuggled next to him as she stared at it all.

"None of these things from the box make me remember anything from our childhood. I don't understand why she placed my name on the security box and I don't know the password. There isn't even a picture in her belongings of the two of us. Not a letter, a note, a diary, nothing that would indicate Annette even had a sister or a family ever." She was frustrated.

"It will come to you. Just relax, take a little break," Hal suggested as he and Jake took seats on the edge of the bed.

Michaela stared at the items, at the bear, her first bear ever, and then the scene. Her heart hammered inside of her chest. It was like a lightbulb went off inside of her head. "Oh God. I'm so stupid." She sat up. "Ouch."

"Easy, Michaela. What's wrong?" Jake asked, placing his hand on her knee.

"I think I got it."

"Really?" Hal asked her.

She pointed to the bear. "Thank you, Billy. Thank you for reminding me about the wishful thoughts of children. Things were so bad in my house. You know we had nothing, no toys, and I explained that Annette cried all the time. We were only children. How did we cope with all the dysfunction, the yelling, the screaming, the hateful words, and the horror of it all?" She stood up, pulled the wine ornament out of the box, and then turned to look at the paining and then back at her three men who watched her with uncertainty but full attention.

"We dreamed of going away, to another place, to a perfect life, together. Away from the pain, the fear, and the negativity. We dreamed of Tuscany." She held the wine ornament up so they could see it.

"I don't understand," Hal said.

"You think Tuscany is the password?" Jake asked.

"It only has seven letters," Billy added.

She shook her head.

"What stood out most to you even though this painting isn't finished?" she asked them.

"The sun," Jake stated and stood up. He smiled at Michaela.

"The Tuscan sun," she said, and he hugged her close.

"That has nine letters. That must be it," Hal said.

She squeezed Jake tight and closed her eyes, feeling the tears again.

"Maybe my sister really was trying to protect me that day, like I had always protected her growing up?"

"Let's call Alonso and see if that password works." Jake pulled out his phone and handed it to Michaela. Her voice sounded shaky as she spoke to him.

"Alonso, try Tuscan sun. Oh, and I want to know what was in that security box. I need to know." She closed the phone and turned in Jake's arms to look at the unfinished painting.

"I'm going to finish that painting, Jake. Before I do anything else to this house, I'm finishing it. For Annette."

Epilogue

A week later Michaela was upstairs in her bedroom finishing the painting. As she added a few last strokes, completing her project with an uplifted heart and a new perspective on life, she sighed. Sitting down on the bed, paintbrush in hand, she absorbed the scene. The beautiful, bright Tuscan sun light cascaded over a lovely home, situated on a vineyard in the distance. It looked so inviting and perfect, just as Annette and she had talked about it being. The home, the family, and the two of them safe and happy. In the corner heading toward the house with two dogs they never had the opportunity to have, two young girls held hands, their excitement evident even though their backs were toward the viewer. Her and Annette. Children making their wish a reality.

She felt the tear roll down her cheek as she recalled what she learned only days before from the items in the security box.

Her sister wrote her a letter. Michaela pulled it from her pocket, having read it multiple times already, and bringing tears to her eyes, yet a joy and closure to her heart.

To the best sister a girl could ask for,

If you're reading this letter, then I'm probably dead. Know that I'm in a happier place than I've ever been before.

I know you probably hate me. There was a time, a long time, that I hated myself. I ran away, unable to handle any of it anymore. But you stayed. You were always so much stronger than me, braver, and more determined to have a future. I gave up, gave in, and took the wrong paths. But when you contacted me the other day, trying to make plans to get back together, something changed inside of me, Michaela. I felt something. It was deep, way inside my heart, a heart I thought was hollow and black.

You called again, left another message. Insistent and stubborn as always, and something changed in me. I remembered those horrible nights, crying, complaining, shivering in fear as the sounds of the yelling, the banging, and things breaking scared me. And I remembered you holding me in your arms telling me that everything was going to be all right. So many times throughout these years after I left, I longed for you to hold me and make things right. But I chose to run and hide, instead of fighting. I'm dying, Michaela. I'm going to die because of the bad choices I made. But I want to make things right.

In this box—I knew you would figure out the password. You were always so smart and beautiful—you'll find my last dying wish. Although I may have done some stupid things to get this money, it was still well earned. And you may not realize it but Solomon really isn't that bad of a person, he's just misguided. Perhaps if he had a sister like you growing up, he wouldn't be where he is now. Either way, it doesn't matter. But telling you how much I love you, and how grateful I was for having you as my sister was important to me.

So, I leave you, my only family, the only person worthy of all I have left in the world, this package of money. Don't worry, my attorney's number along with a copy of the will is in the box, too. No one but you can get this. I want you to take that trip, Michaela. I want you to go and see the Tuscan sun. I want you to think of me, of us there together at peace, and filled with happiness. I love you always. There are no regrets, no more pain, and no more sadness now. Just fond memories of that Tuscan sun that helped us to survive.

All my love. Oh, and have a glass of wine for me.

Your little sister,

Annette

Michaela wiped away the tear and looked at the painting. She would do as her sister asked, and she would take that trip. Heck, with the quarter of a million dollars her sister left her, she could take a lot of trips.

"Hey, you finished it?" Jake asked as he entered her bedroom. She wiped her eyes and folded up the letter they were used to seeing her with, and stood up.

"It's finished," she whispered.

Billy and Hal entered next.

"Oh wow, Michaela, it's gorgeous. You are so talented," Billy told her.

She smiled. "I'm glad it's complete. I feel just about fully relieved and free again."

"Just about? Why not completely? The bad guys have all been locked up. Carlucci gave up Dipero's location while trying to minimize the charges against him thanks to those thumb drives. The Feds have their work cut out for them weeding through all the documented corruption and so does Alonso. There was a nice list of important names on those thumb drives, but none of that has anything to do wit us. Nothing else is connected to you, so there's no more danger, and your sister left you that letter and all that money," Jake said.

She looked at her men.

"Well, you three need to commit to a date so we can take that trip to Italy. No more excuses of fear of flying and not fitting in. I need you," she whispered, knowing that whenever she said that to her men, they immediately succumbed to her desires.

Hal pointed his finger at her, and then curled it indicating for her to come closer to him as he stood by the bed.

She walked over and he grabbed her by the waist, twisted her around, and placed her over his thighs.

"Hal!" she squealed.

The feel of his large hand caressing over her ass through her cotton shorts aroused her.

"Someone has been taking advantage of her men. I think you need a little reminder about who's in charge."

"Hal, don't you—"

Smack.

She jerked as his hand came down on her ass for the first time ever. For weeks they'd teased her, threatened her with spankings when she was naughty or stubborn, and now here she was over his knees and completely aroused by the sensations it caused.

"Not so mouthy now, is she?" Billy asked as Hal lifted her back up and into his arms on his lap.

"I don't deserve a spanking." She pouted.

"I thought differently. Now, this is the deal. We are going to go with you to Tuscany, but when we return, we want a commitment from you, too," Hal stated. She looked at him oddly, and then at Jake and Billy who stood there looking so sexy and handsome. She loved them so very much.

"What commitment are you referring to?"

Hal caressed her thigh with his hand as she remained sitting across his lap.

"The one where you ask us to move in with you, so we can spend more time together."

She felt the tears fill her eyes. Her place was much bigger than theirs and it was closer to the beach and boardwalk. After all the work she'd done on it, she didn't want to sell it or leave here.

"Really? You would give up your house to move in here with me?" she asked.

"We'd still hold on to the house to use as rental income," Billy said.

"Yeah, that's all we need to do, start letting people think that our woman is taking care of us financially. Not happening," Jake stated with his arms crossed in front of his chest.

She chuckled. "No one knows anything about the money but you three. Well, I don't need to wait until after Tuscany. Move in with me now. Stay here with me so that we can begin every day together and end every night together."

"Now that's one hell of an offering. Yes," Hal said and then kissed her.

"Yes," Jake stated and then leaned down and kissed her next.

"Yes, only on one condition," Billy said.

"One condition? What?" she asked, wondering what he could possibly ask for.

"You put that huge-ass teddy bear on the floor, and move it out of my spot in the bed."

She chuckled as she looked over Hal's shoulder and saw the bear sitting right in the middle of the bed.

"I don't know, I kind of like him there. Can't he join us?" she teased, and Hal tipped her body over pretending to drop her and she squealed. Billy lifted her up and into his arms. She straddled his waist.

"There's only one bear allowed in your bed, baby, and that's me."

Billy kissed her deeply and then lowered her to the bed where Jake and Hal quickly divested her of her clothing. The bear was tossed onto the floor, and soon she was surrounded by her gloriously sexy, naked men who once again set her heart on fire, with a love she hoped would last forever.

THE END

WWW.DIXIELYNNDWYER.COM

ABOUT THE AUTHOR

People seem to be more interested in my name than where I get my ideas for my stories from. So I might as well share the story behind my name with all my readers.

My momma was born and raised in New Orleans. At the age of twenty, she met and fell in love with an Irishman named Patrick Riley Dwyer. Needless to say, the family was a bit taken aback by this as they hoped she would marry a family friend. It was a modern day arranged marriage kind of thing and my momma downright refused.

Being that my momma's families were descendents of the original English speaking Southerners, they wanted the family blood line to stay pure. They were wealthy and my father's family was poor.

Despite attempts by my grandpapa to make Patrick leave and destroy the love between them, my parents married. They recently celebrated their sixtieth wedding anniversary.

I am one of six children born to Patrick and Lynn Dwyer. I am a combination of both Irish and a true Southern belle. With a name like Dixie Lynn Dwyer it's no wonder why people are curious about my name.

Just as my parents had a love story of their own, I grew up intrigued by the lifestyles of others. My imagination as well as my need to stray from the straight and narrow made me into the woman I am today.

For all titles by Dixie Lynn Dwyer, please visit
www.bookstrand.com/dixie-lynn-dwyer

Siren Publishing, Inc.
www.SirenPublishing.com

Lightning Source UK Ltd.
Milton Keynes UK
UKHW02f1444070318
319039UK00006B/962/P